The Book of

Esau

Also from the Langley Press:

Mary Ann Cotton: Victorian Serial Killer
Victorian Durham
In Search of the Little Count
The Bishopric of Durham
Severin: A Tale of Jack the Ripper
Crippen's Secret

For free downloads and more from the Langley
Press, please visit our website at
http://tinyurl.com/lpdirect.

The cover shows an anonymous photograph of an
Indian Elephant, c. 1860 (Getty Museum)

The Book of

Esau

A Murder Mystery of
Victorian Durham

by Simon Webb

Chapter I

A police ambulance was already standing outside the house when I arrived. The trim little mare that had been detailed to pull it seemed to have a sense of the grimness of the situation. She hung her head. As I approached, a uniformed constable stepped into the gaslight and touched the front of his helmet.

'I'm going to need your help, officer,' I said.

It was hard work, lugging the big whole-plate camera and the wooden tripod up those stairs. As I entered the room where the dead man was, I was alarmed to find myself alone with him: the constable had left the tripod on the landing and returned to his post at the front door. Somehow, I had expected someone else to be in attendance in the upstairs room.

I felt that I should greet the dead man in some way, as one does when one enters an occupied room. Instead I stood, dumbfounded, at the threshold, then set to work trying to assemble my equipment as quietly as possible. I still don't know what made me think that I should try to be quiet.

I did not recognise the dead man at first. His beard had gone – indeed there were fresh scratches about his chin where the razor had caught. He had assumed someone else's clothes. In fact he looked as if he had burst out of the clothes he was wearing: they were all too small for him.

His eyes had lost the glitter of life and looked like eyes fashioned out of mother of pearl. His lips were blue and bloodless. His expression was blank, unrevealing. His hands had the colour and sheen of a pale cheese.

Some blood had penetrated through his shirt and jacket, and dried to a colour that seemed near to black in the gas-lit room. Though I looked closely, I could see no hole in his clothes near that point – had he received his death-blow while naked, and had he had time to dress afterwards? If he had bled to death, I thought, then surely there would be more blood? And if he had been bleeding to death, surely he could not have calmly composed himself in his easy chair?

It seemed that he had even found time to rest his cane against the chair in such a way that he could use it to help himself stand up. But he would never stand up again – that was evident.

The cane, with its tip carved in the shape of a wolf's head, would stay in place while I photographed everything. It would remain leaning against the side of the chair when four policemen took the dead body downstairs to the ambulance.

After what seemed an age, but was perhaps only a minute or two, the large form of Detective Inspector Albert Maitland joined me in the room, and at last I was no longer alone with the body.

On reflection, I think that I felt a little more than just compassion for the dead man, and curiosity about his death. I felt sorry for myself, and for the whole of creation, which is subject to such an end. Before the night when I saw him dead, death had been purely theoretical for me. My labours on that night in 1895 brought me face to face with the reality of it.

I first encountered Esau Harrison when I was walking up Claypath in the city of Durham. It was an icy day in the January of 1895 and I was planning to buy some photographic chemicals from a pharmacist up there. A young lady was standing in the street near the shop, wearing a long black coat and a red beret. She was gazing into the shop with a mild smile on her lips.

As I approached, I heard the undeniable sound of glass breaking inside the shop, mixed with loud speech in a deep voice, and cries of 'murder' from a high, panicky voice. I hastened to the door but as I neared it, the pharmacist flew out. I say 'flew' out because, for a split second, he was flying, in the strictest sense, because no part of his body was touching the ground. He turned over in the air and landed on his back, quite winded.

As he tried to get up, his body started to half-roll, half-slide down the steep street. He was followed on his trajectory by two large bottles of a clear liquid – these smashed, and the liquid spread down the icy pavement. I looked to the door to see who was doing all this, expecting to see some tough or hooligan. Instead I saw Esau Harrison himself for the first time – a tall broad gentleman with a white-flecked red beard.

He came through the street door of the pharmacy, a cane stuck through his belt like a sword. He drew the cane and began to use it in the usual way, as an aid to walking. He was not discomposed, or ruffled in any way. The young lady in the beret took his arm and they proceeded down the street. I ran up behind the man and was about to seize his shoulder. Instead, he whirled round and I felt his cane in my chest.

'What is the meaning of this?' I asked, my anger slightly tempered by the fact that Harrison looked to be some kind of gentleman.

'The meaning of this is *judgement*,' Harrison replied, in an unfamiliar accent. His giant build reminded me of my father-in-law, Inspector Albert Maitland. I judged that it would be foolish to offer him any violence. Harrison turned and continued down the street with his companion.

I heard the pharmacist groaning behind me, and went to assist him. 'What happened here?' I asked.

'Nothing at all, young Jacob,' he replied. We stepped into the comparative warmth of the shop, our feet sliding over broken glass. Somebody had broken the glass-topped counter of the shop, as well as a glazed inner door and several large medicine bottles.

'Nothing?' I echoed, gazing around me.

'I had a disagreement with that gentleman. That is all.'

'He threw you out of your own shop!'

'I ran out to get some fresh air,' he offered feebly, kicking some of the glass on the floor into a corner.

'Who broke all this glass?'

'An accident.'

'You must report him to the police. He's a maniac.'

'No need. No harm done.'

When the pharmacist had supplied me with the chemicals I needed, I made my way back down Claypath, shaking my head, and back into the city.

On Framwellgate Bridge, I saw Harrison again. My rage at having been poked in the chest by the man suddenly rose up; but of course it was too late now. I had a sense, from the pharmacist's words, that there was more to the incident on Claypath than had at first appeared: perhaps the shopkeeper had done something wrong, and Harrison had punished him. That would explain the pharmacist's lack of anger at the expensive damage done to his premises.

I knew that there were ways in which a pharmacist could cause offence – by supplying poisons without keeping a record of the purchasers, for instance, or by adulterating drugs. Nevertheless, I couldn't help thinking that Harrison should have applied to the police, rather than taking what he called 'judgement' into his own brawny hands.

Of course, I then reasoned, if the pharmacist were to be found guilty of something in a court of law, he could easily die, as many men did, during a five-year stint of hard labour. Perhaps a good throwing, and some destruction of his property, constituted a more humane punishment.

I observed Harrison's broad back from a distance and decided to have as little to do with him as possible in future. As I thought all this, Harrison was walking ahead of me, arm-in-arm with the young lady.

Harrison was the kind of man who would catch anyone's attention. On his head, he wore a smoking-hat, complete with tassel hanging down, and with complex oriental embroidery on it. In itself the hat was not odd, but in those days it was unknown for a man to wear one of those brimless, dome-shaped hats out of doors. It gave his head a faint resemblance to that of some eastern potentate, or even one of the Liverpool Chinese.

The rest of the man's clothes were scarcely less remarkable. He wore a suit of thin, fawn-coloured linen, and tan shoes of such lightweight leather that they creased like kid gloves. Such skimpy clothing seemed truly bizarre at a time when the river under the bridge was frozen, and the stranger's thin-soled shoes were crunching on two inches of snow. Despite his lack of suitable covering, the gentleman (for such he appeared to be) was not shivering. His nose was not red, and he showed no sign of wanting to hurry to some warm destination. He showed absolutely nothing in his demeanour to show that he had just attacked a pharmacist. He was truly a strange sight, and I was not the only person on the bridge who was looking at him in surprise.

I told all this to my wife when I returned to our combined house and shop on Elvet Bridge.

My wife's maiden name had been Hebe Maitland. Having been raised a Quaker, I had had to be baptised into the Anglican Church to marry her, which my Quaker mother had accepted with the epistolatory equivalent of a patient shrug. I had been instructed in the rudiments of my new denomination by the eccentric Dr Considine, who was now preparing me for the ritual of Confirmation.

At that period of our marriage, Hebe had a coquettish little phrase that she liked to use in our conversations. She would say, 'Oh! Now I see how our marriage will end up!' and she would half-turn her head away from me. The business of half-turning her head was a comically ambiguous gesture in itself. It served to present her lovely profile to me, an aspect of her person that she knew I adored. I had frequently experimented with photographs and silhouettes of this profile.

A new refinement of the 'Oh! Now I see how our marriage will end up!' phrase comprised her recent attempts to apply it to some incongruous situation. As a response to my description of the man in the fawn suit the phrase did indeed seem incongruous. Seeing that I was puzzled, she went on to explain; 'You never notice anything *I* wear, yet you come home with a complete description of the clothes of a man you have never seen before. And of his daughter's clothes to boot, which is worse.'

Of course, when she turned her profile to me, there was nothing to do but kiss her cheek. When I had kissed it, and breathed in her delicious smell of flour and soap, she then cryptically uttered the word 'Norwegian'.

I asked her what she meant.

'The man must be a Norwegian,' she explained. 'We have lots of Norwegian visitors up here, either on business missions, or as tourists. Norway is very cold, so these Norwegians will probably find it quite warm here, even at this time of year. Hence the very thin clothing. He would need nothing more.'

'But his daughter was very well wrapped up,' I said.

'Perhaps she is delicate,' Hebe replied.

On the Thursday of the next week, Hebe and I went by train to Newcastle, where Hebe was able to buy some new clothes. She assured me in advance that I would certainly fail to notice these clothes when she first wore them. The weekends were the busiest times for our business, so that any pleasure trip we took tended to happen on weekdays. At these times my uncle Eadweard, senior partner in the photography firm, would take over the shop. On this Thursday, when we returned with our parcels, he reported that he had sold a reasonable amount of celluloid roll film, glass plates, printing paper, chemicals and postcards, and had even taken a portrait photograph of a foreign gentleman.

'Funny chap,' he said. 'Insisted on putting his chin down and staring straight into the camera. Only wanted his head in the picture as well. It's going to be an odd sort of portrait. It'll be all eyes, goggling out like fried eggs. He even put some drops in his eyes before I took the picture.'

'Was he alone?' I asked.

'No. He was with your friend Tiger.'

'Tiger Terris?'

'Aye. And the funny thing was, Terris was sober.'

'Oh come, Uncle,' I protested. 'He's not always drunk.'

'That may be so,' my uncle replied, 'but he's certainly not always sober. Not in the afternoon, anyway.'

I couldn't really argue with this. 'Did you use the big plate camera?' I asked, referring to our venerable portrait workhorse.

'No. Couldn't. He wants it made up into twenty-five postcards. Had to use the half-plate. Even so there'll be a big margin round 'em.' I thanked my uncle for standing in for me, and wished him a good evening.

Most of our developing and printing was done at night. The cellar where we did it could not be fully blacked out during the day, and in any case the photographer was likely to be disturbed down there when the sun was up – the darkroom shared the basement with a small kitchen and the coal cellar. I found the half-plate that my uncle had exposed, carefully sealed in its lightproof case. I donned my apron and prepared the chemical baths needed to develop the latent image.

The picture that gradually appeared in the developing solution was not blurred, and the exposure looked perfect. It was, however, just as odd a portrait as my uncle had predicted. What was more surprising was that it was a portrait of the same fawn-suited man I had noticed on Framwellgate Bridge during the previous week.

He was staring out of the picture with very great concentration and intensity. As a photographer, I have always tried to stop people staring into the lens – when they do so their eyes become too large and they tend to look mad or drunk. I like them to gaze off into the distance, or to look at some beloved person (unseen through the viewfinder) such as a wife or child who might be with them in the studio. This makes for a formal, but also warm, portrait. The portrait of the man in the fawn suit was not warm, but challenging. Those eyes seemed to draw in the viewer. I quickly made twenty-six photographic postcards of the portrait and went to bed.

My uncle Eadweard dropped by the next morning, to see if I had any prints of the portrait. I gave him my extra copy and he gazed at it a long time without speaking. Then he said, 'Never seen owt like it. Looks like a git dead fish.' (At times of excitement, my uncle Eadweard would easily slip into the Durham dialect he had learned at my grandmother's knee.) The eyes of Esau Harrison did indeed have some of the naked directness of the eyes of a dead fish on a slab. We were to learn, however, that the subject of the portrait had a great deal of life in him.

Chapter II

The account books of Blount & Blount, photographers, show that Mr Esau Harrison ordered over one hundred postcards of his portrait in the next few months. If the postcards were to be used as *cartes de visite*, one had to assume that Harrison was visiting a great many people. In fact, it later transpired that he was not using them as *cartes de visite* in the usual sense.

The backs of the cards were all stamped with the name and address of our little business, and soon people who had not been given a card by Harrison himself were trying to buy them from us. They asked for the picture of 'Professor Harrison,' 'Dr Harrison' or 'The American Professor.' Since my uncle had not encountered many Americans, he had been unable to identify Harrison's accent. We did not supply our visitors with these pictures, since we felt that Harrison's image should be his own to distribute.

Harrison had become a celebrity in our

picturesque little city. He had been giving a series of lectures on various subjects at a number of venues in the area. He lectured on 'The Secrets of Health' in a Methodist church hall, on 'The Dangers of Alcohol' in the Quaker Meeting House and on 'The Persistence of the Soul' in a ballroom in North Road. He also lectured on 'Pythagoras and the transmutation of souls'. He claimed to be a fully qualified doctor of medicine and indeed a teacher of other physicians in the United States. He was very vague on exactly where in that vast country he came from, but this didn't seem to bother his followers.

The lectures were free, but a bag was passed round at the end for contributions. To my surprise, I learned that my friend Tiger had attended all of these lectures, and that it was often he who took the collecting-bag round. It is possible, given his talents as a speaker, that Harrison could collect more money via contributions than by charging a fixed admission. He was gaining followers daily, and word got around that he was trying to book a very large venue for his next talk.

Two weeks before his lecture on the subject of 'The Soul and the Body', small posters appeared all over the City of Durham and in several villages nearby. The posters featured an engraved version of my uncle's photographic portrait of Harrison, with a text promising:

An educational lecture on the relationship of the soul to the body: how the body can leave the soul without death ensuing: how drugs beneficial to the body can be deleterious to the soul: how true health can only be obtained by treating the soul and the body together.

The lecture was to take place at the theatre in Saddler Street on a Monday afternoon. The size of the theatre, which had some five hundred seats, and the expense Harrison must have incurred to hire it and print the posters, suggested that the American now had a very large following, and was confident of filling the place.

Reading the poster, it occurred to me that if Harrison had once been a respected physician, he may have lost his place because of his fondness for the supernatural. Most doctors in England had long ago given up looking to spiritual matters for causes and cures. Letting my eye roll over the phrase *'treating the soul and body together'* I began to wonder if Harrison advocated exorcism – a procedure that had once been very popular in Christian churches, and had even been used by the Founder of the Christian Church himself.

I had no more intention of attending this

Monday afternoon lecture than I had had of attending any of the others. Durham was then awash with public lectures of all different kinds: lecturers from the University, and amateurs in every field of knowledge, tried to supplement their incomes in this way.

I liked to attend talks on hard scientific subjects such as chemistry, engineering and geology. I had attended a series of public lectures on the subject of evolution – an idea that was still quite controversial in those days. The lecturer, a follower of Darwin and Huxley, had promised his audience sight of 'accurate casts of skulls of the various types of primitive men, with some casts of the skulls of the higher apes.' The threat of this exhibition of carrion was what kept Hebe away from that particular lecture.

The lecturer on evolution was obviously well-informed, but he had no idea of how to present a show to the public. He had his entire collection of plaster skulls ranged on a table at the start of the lecture, so that there was no expectation attached to the business of seeing any of them. He seemed to be slightly confused about which skull was which, and should really have labelled them, discreetly, in advance. I was pleased that Hebe had not attended this lecture: when the lecturer held up the skull of 'an idiot who died but a few weeks ago' I knew that Hebe might have been very upset at that point. Certainly, the skull was very different from the skull of the normal modern human with which the lecturer compared it. The idiot's skull sloped back from his brows at a forty-five degree angle. Had this been a primitive man born too late? Both Darwin and my lecturer seemed to entertain this possibility.

In the end I was persuaded, rather against my will, to go to Esau Harrison's 'body and soul' lecture, by my friend Tiger who was, like me, a member of the illustrious Chemical Club of Durham. In fact it was after a meeting of the club that Allan 'Tiger' Terris explained to me, in rather bizarre terms, why he was very keen to hear Esau Harrison speak at the theatre.

Terris was by far the most famous member of the Chemical Club, though I must say that his grasp of chemistry was very slight. He was not widely known by his actual name, but rather by the heroic nickname, 'Tiger Terris'. Some time in the 80s, the local newspapers had 'boosted' him as the brave Durham Light Infantryman, of the second battalion then in India, who had fought a tiger and lost his hand. After close reading, it was clear that what had really happened was not quite so heroic. Terris was not in fact in uniform when the tiger bit him, and the tiger was already dying, with a brain full of shot. If Terris had had decent medical attention he would have kept his hand. Unfortunately, he had been on leave in a native province when he was bitten. The wounds became infected and the hand had to be amputated.

Although the injury had taken place during a tiger hunt, Terris had not been holding a gun, but rather a box brownie. He was an amateur photographer, and as such qualified to be a member of the Chemical Club when he returned to his home town of Durham. Carelessly dressed, though in expensive clothes, Terris still cultivated large black military whiskers. Thanks to their distinctive shape, he was often recognised by admirers in the streets.

Tiger Terris explained his interest in Harrison's lecture as I walked back with him from the meeting to his father's house in Old Elvet.

The meeting of the Chemical Club that we had both just attended had started with an *agenda* (that is, a large jug of ale) and had worked through the agenda with great thoroughness. Some *points of order* (glasses of grog) had been raised. After three hours, the meeting room (a private room at the Half Moon Public House) was vacated in an orderly fashion after *any other business* (last orders).

Tiger had taken little liquid refreshment

during the meeting, preferring to suck on a series of small cigars.

He was generally pretty ebullient at these events. When the agenda had been read, he would usually *read out a report* (sing a comic song with all the accompanying gestures). Tiger refused to do so that night, and his place was taken by the enthusiastic but tone-deaf barrister, Harburton. Tiger Terris seemed much more thoughtful than usual, and I saw him frowning at his own thoughts. Though asked several times to read a report, he steadfastly declined to do so.

'This fellow Harrison says that the soul is the same shape as the body. He says that a ghost is really the soul, divested of the body,' he added as we approached his home.

'S'interesting,' I said. 'But wassit got to do with you?' We had stopped at what Tiger called 'his Governor's' and were leaning on the painted stone pillars that stood to the right and left of the front door. The unaccustomed frown gathered on Tiger's brow again.

'I've never told you this, Jacob,' he said, his face so close to mine that my own face was bathed in steam, 'But you are my dearest friend, old chap, and I think I should tell you. You see, the fact is, *my hand is still there*.' I was tired, and rather drunk, but the macabre idea he had introduced into our conversation made me sober up.

'You mean, the hand you lost?' I asked. On reflection, this was a very stupid question.

'Yes,' he said. 'To the rational mind I left it in India. I suppose it was burned up in the hospital incinerator. That's a conflagration I've often seen in my dreams, I can tell you. Oh yes, I dream about that furnace, though I never saw it. But in my dream, the hand is still attached, you see. The native stoker shoves it in and shuts the furnace door, *on my wrist*. It's a pretty tough dream, old chap.' He smiled mirthlessly and put his heel on the boot-scraper by the door.

'To the rational mind, yes, my hand is gone,' he continued. 'Oh, and I know you can't see it any more; neither can I. But I can still *feel* it, every minute of every day. And I tell you, Jacob, at night it *hurts*. And not just in my dreams.' I gazed at him in amazement for some seconds. I had never had any inkling of this before.

'Have you mentioned this to your father?' I asked. His father was a wealthy and respected doctor in the town.

'Oh yes,' he said. 'My old Governor says it's a 'phantom' hand. He says servicemen and labourers who lose a hand nearly always feel they still have it. He says I should count myself lucky that I still have the rest of the arm.'

'So what treatment does he suggest?'

'None. There isn't any treatment. Not with our English 'rational' medicine. But perhaps this Yank knows something my old Governor doesn't. Perhaps the hand I can still feel is my soul's hand, and it's sick and in pain. Perhaps this Yankee can do something about it.'

As he said this, my friend Tiger Terris seemed to be glowing with optimism. I felt ashamed: I was so drunk that my thoughts on his predicament were too slow to be of use. I had been determined to make a 'good night' of it, and had failed to act on his unusually serious mood. I patted him clumsily on the shoulder, then bade him goodnight, having first promised to come with him to the lecture.

The theatre on Saddler Street had recently been refurbished. It looked very smart, with new red velvet on its seats and gold-embroidered curtains hanging on either side of the small stage. It seemed strange to be going into a theatre on a weekday afternoon, and even stranger to have no tickets, and to have to part with no money on the way in. The overwhelming majority in the audience were women, and of those most were women of the leisured classes. I recognised some obvious bluestockings, some old maids, and widows of all ages. I think that some of these were counted among Harrison's devoted disciples in the city. They seemed to be ecstatic to be there in the theatre, even though Harrison was nowhere to be seen.

In contrast to the women at the front, the back rows of the stalls were taken up by students of the Durham University, in their academic gowns and caps. The students seemed to be in very high spirits. They were pushing each other off their seats, hiding their heads in their gowns, and flamboyantly smoking cigarettes.

Tiger arrived later than me, in his best suit, and so excited that he couldn't even say hello. An usher found us seats right at the front. Tiger had an aisle seat. I looked around and saw Harrison's young female companion, still in her red beret, sitting just across the central aisle from us. As if the ushers had been waiting for us and us alone, the doors were closed as we sat down. I expected the house lights to be dimmed and the stage-lights to come up, but that didn't happen.

With the entire auditorium equally well lit, Esau Harrison entered, not from the wings, but from the back of the stalls. His lady disciples, turning their heads, straightened their backs and smoothed down their dresses at the sight of him. He worked his way along the aisle, shaking hands and patting shoulders, saying a few words to some of the people he greeted. Evidently, many members of the audience were 'regulars' at these events. There was enthusiastic applause as Harrison approached the stage. He was now wearing, not a fawn linen suit, but another linen suit, of pale blue. This clothing was nowhere near warm enough for the northern city of Durham. Even in August, the cold wind can rise from the river, and people dart across the bridges as if they feared hidden snipers.

A question arose in my mind as to how Esau Harrison, a man not in the first flush of youth, intended to get onto the stage from the aisle. The stage was waist-high to him, and there were no steps. He answered my question in the most remarkable fashion. After a short run, he grasped the edge of the stage, and then sprang upwards with his legs. He turned over in the air and landed with his knees bent.

As he turned round, a burst of applause rose up, which he quieted with a raised hand. In the gathering silence, he walked to the edge of the stage, and then, for the first time, I noticed the strangeness of his gait. In the seat that I occupied, my eyes were roughly level with his ankles. This gave me an excellent viewpoint for the examination of his legs, his feet and his style of walking. He seemed to me to walk with his knees and feet pointing out, and he stood with his heels off the ground. He took some pains to disguise this peculiarity, but seated thus low down I could not help but notice it. He also seemed to me to move his head from side to side more that most people as he walked, but I think this is something I first noticed at a later date.

At the beginning of his lecture, he mentioned his athletic feat of jumping onto the stage to illustrate the point he wanted to make. He was a man of sixty years of age, he said, and yet his knees and ankles were as springy as rubber, his bones as tough as steel. This was not due to any very freakish diet (though Harrison admitted that he was a vegetarian), nor was it due to an expensive patent medicine. It was because he had paid attention to the health of his soul.

Tiger listened to this with total concentration, absently scratching the stump of his missing hand. His mouth was open, his eyes unblinking. He looked like a sensitive child watching a Punch and Judy show for the first time, completely 'taken in' by the whole experience. I had never seen such concentration in him before. He was generally far too easily distracted from any activity, even rowing a boat, and in conversation would either rattle away like a madman or fall asleep.

Harrison was certainly a very good speaker. He had no lectern, nor notes to put on it. He prowled about the stage, addressing different parts of the audience by turns. His voice was rich, deep and flowing, and his American accent gave it a sense of novelty. Public lectures in Durham tended to be delivered in either a half-disguised Durham dialect, or in the upper-class accent of the typical academic, cleric or dilettante. I should add that nothing about Harrison's voice or person suggested a Norwegian origin.

He spoke for about ten minutes, which was the time it took for the students at the back of the stalls to organise their claque. There was a stirring behind me, and I looked round to see a comically skinny student with a baton stand up in his seat and gesture for the rest of the students to rise. Under the gas house-lights their faces expressed a variety of things, from drunken bravado to utter panic. As Harrison watched, his face devoid of expression, they began to sing, to the tune of *God Save the Queen*:

Here comes old Harrison
Long live old Harrison
Here comes old Harrison

Here comes old Harrison
Here comes old Harrison

Here comes old Harrison
Here comes old Harrison.

It looked as if the students intended to sing this repetitive and unpatriotic ditty for some considerable time. An elderly lady, in *pince-nez* and bombazine, stood up and waved her glass-topped stick at them. It was clear that she was shouting something, but the students were warming to their task and getting louder. I didn't hear a word of the old lady's. Harrison himself looked down at her from the stage, and I thought I saw the smallest shadow of a smile deep inside his beard. Other followers of Harrison were now on their feet, and an elderly usher occupied himself in trying to dissuade a short fat man, evidently a Harrisonite, from fighting the students.

While all this commotion was going on behind him, Tiger Terris never took his eyes off the target of all this irony, the speaker. With great coolness, Esau Harrison took something from his pocket, which I quickly recognised as one of the photographic postcards made for him by Blount & Blount. He took a pencil from another pocket and scribbled something on the back of the card. He crouched down and handed it to Tiger, which was in itself evidence of his great physical suppleness. He then stood up, bowed, and calmly vanished into the wings of the stage. Tiger showed me the card. On the back somebody had put Harrison's address in Durham, using a rubber address stamp of the sort that any decent stationer can make up. This sat above the address of Blount & Blount. Under his own address, Harrison had written *come and see me tonight*.

Chapter III

'He says he doesn't mind about those students mocking him. He says they were put up to it by their teachers. He says that half the clerics in the city have been preaching against him in their sermons. He says most of those students were students of theology. They're just pawns of the Church of England. He says they're being taught all the wrong stuff about religion. He says he could teach them more in an evening than the University could teach them in a lifetime. And I believe him.'

Tiger Terris had come to the shop very late that night and found me working in the darkroom downstairs. I offered him some of the cheap port I kept on the shelf in a chemical-bottle but, to my surprise, he refused it. He also refused a cigarette. He went through the partition into our little kitchen and poured himself a glass of water, of all things.

'Have you been talking to Harrison all this time?' I asked. 'It's nearly eleven. You went down there at eight.'

'No no,' he answered. 'I've been moving my things.'

'Moving your things? What things?'

'Oh, you know, my clothes and what-have-you…'

'You mean you're moving house?'

'That's right. I can't live with the old Governor any more, I'm afraid.'

'But where are you moving to?' I was standing gazing at him, holding a pair of wooden developing tongs. Behind me, in a chemical bath, the photograph of an old lady was rapidly going completely black.

Tiger had always lived with his father, except when he had been on military service elsewhere. True, his irregular habits evidently caused friction between father and son, but to move out so precipitately?

'Where are you moving to?' I asked.

'I'm moving in with Harrison, of course!'

'With Harrison?'

'Oh yes. He has quite a big flat. And he needs an assistant, you see. But he needs someone who can work with him any time of the day or night.'

'He needs an assistant? So he's going to pay you?'

'Oh yes. But that's the interesting bit. He won't pay me in money. He knows I'd just spend it on the things that are bad for me. He's going to pay me in kind.'

In retrospect, considering the amount of money found with Harrison's corpse, I am sure that the American's failure to pay my friend could not have arisen from impecuniousness. It was either miserliness, or a real concern about what Tiger would spend his money on. At the time, my ears pricked up, and I thought I could detect sharp practice.

Meanwhile, I was so interested in Tiger's news that the print of the old lady had gone black all over, and now looked like a rectangular hole in the bottom of the developing-tray. 'How will he pay you in kind?' I asked. 'Will it be beads, or sea-shells?'

'Oh of course not,' said Tiger, still very good-humoured. 'He's going to cure me.'

'Of what?'

'My pain. The pain I feel in the hand that I don't have anymore. The hand I left in India. He's started already.'

'Started what?'

'The cure of course.'

'So what does he do?'

'It's mesmerism.'

'What?'

'Mesmerism.'

Tiger left shortly after he had conveyed this interesting piece of information. I didn't know whether to laugh or cry.

Mesmerism! Animal magnetism! The eighteenth century conjuring trick that had captivated Europe! After a period in the doldrums, the art of the magnetiser was becoming fashionable again at that time. There was also a rising interest in Spiritualism, fortune-telling and straightforward faith healing. There had even been public lectures in favour of these notions in Durham.

Since I thought of myself as a minor sort of scientist, working in the fields of optics and chemistry, I habitually pooh-poohed such notions. Why give up your free will to a sinister 'magnetiser'? How and why should the dead come down to speak to the living? Why should people try to read the future, when it was their own proper job to try to make it? When medicine was advancing so steadily, why put faith in charlatans who 'cured' the same shamming actor ten times a week?

On the whole, I regarded mesmerism as a foolish party game. It was supposed to be a technique whereby susceptible subjects fell completely under the power of the magnetic adept. I had to acknowledge that there did seem to me to be at least 'something in it': I'd heard how chickens could be hypnotised by making them stare along a straight line drawn in the dirt. I had also heard how some dogs became so hypnotised by nothing more than a bowl of water, that they would forget to blink and end up with tears running down their noses.

I also associated Mesmerism with Mesmer's own notorious abuse of his power over his subjects. Apparently, this clever Austrian would 'magnetise' trees, and persuade his followers to cling to the trunks to cure themselves. He did not adopt such an indirect approach with attractive young lady patients, however. Mesmer was dogged by scandal for much of his life. Was this American, Harrison, just another Mesmer?

I went to bed that night feeling very uneasy about my friend Tiger. I was also determined to keep a close eye on him while he was living with the American. Esau Harrison might be up to something very nasty in the lovely Cathedral city of Durham: I didn't want my poor friend to be associated with any scandal. I went to sleep with the happy thought in my head that if a dozen dirty-necked students could prevent Esau Harrison from speaking, then perhaps he was not such a threat to anyone.

Chapter IV

Some weeks after Harrison's abortive lecture at the theatre, I expected a brief visit from my old friend and mentor Mr Broadlock, a man who was in many ways responsible for my liberty and happiness.

In my home town of Croydon, I had fallen in with a rather disreputable young man, whom I will call Jacky. After a visit to a travelling fair on the aptly named Fairfield, where we had seen, among other things, the hairy 'wild man of Borneo', I had gone with Jacky to what he said was his own house. It turned out that it was the house of Mr Broadlock, a celebrated QC. Jacky had tricked me into accompanying him on a burglary.

Of course, Broadlock came in and caught me red-handed, while Jacky got away.

I suppose the eminent QC had seen many young lives ruined by prison, and he did not take me along to the police station. Instead, he insisted, after consulting with my parents, that I should live with my Uncle Eadweard for a year, far to the north,in Durham, so as to avoid corrupting company in Croydon. A year turned into a decade, and to date I have hardly been back to Croydon at all.

This was to be Broadlock's first visit to the North Country, and he was to bring his new wife with him. I looked forward to seeing them both. It appeared that their visit was to be part of their honeymoon, and that the couple were to proceed further north after a short stay in Durham. Broadlock's new wife had family in Newcastle, and they intended to stay with them.

Mr Broadlock had informed me by letter of the time when his train would arrive. I waited on the platform on that bright but chilly day, remembering from my first journey north how fine Durham looked through a train window. The trains, then as now, flew over the massive arches of a railway viaduct, arches that dwarfed the little Durham shops and houses sheltering under them. The Norman Cathedral is an unmistakeable landmark for the city, telling the traveller to gather his things and proceed to a door.

As soon as I recognised Mr Broadlock emerging from the train, it was clear to me that some kind of emergency was in progress. He was holding what I first took to be a bolt of pale pink silk in his arms. As he came out into the light of the station platform I saw that he was actually holding a young woman. She looked to me to be quite dead, although I had never seen a dead human body at that time.

'Help me get her into a cab,' Broadlock cried, recognising me straight away. 'Get sixpence out of my trouser pocket and give it to that porter. Tell him to take our luggage to the County Hotel. Tell him my name.'

The queue of people waiting for cabs behind the station politely stood aside when Mr Broadlock appeared. The look of his wife, with purple shadows under her eyes and a rasping sound in her breath, made them stand back further than was really necessary. They obviously feared that she had some kind of communicable infection. We managed to arrange Mrs Broadlock in the front seat of the cab, under Mr Broadlock's long coat. I volunteered to sit on the floor of the cab in such a way that my back would prevent her falling down. 'What's wrong with her?' I asked, with my knees under my chin.

'Asthma,' he replied. 'And don't worry – it's not infectious.' I had vaguely heard of this condition.

'Is there a decent doctor in this city?' he asked as we trundled down the steep slope from the station.

'Oh yes,' I said. 'Dr Terris is the father of a friend of mine. All the best people go to him. I'm sure he'll be able to cure her.'

'I'd be very surprised to see him do that,' said Broadlock with a wintry smile. 'It's thought to be incurable. One treats the symptoms and prays for fewer attacks.'

'And this is an attack?' I asked.

'It is.'

At the County Hotel, which overlooks the river from a position very near our shop, I ran to get Dr Terris while Broadlock carried his wife up to their room. Dr Terris was, happily, at home, and he had only to fetch his doctor's bag from his study and walk with me, shrugging on his jacket as he walked. 'Asthma?' he asked. 'Well, we'll see about that. Those fancy London doctors can be wrong, you know.'

'But what is it, this asthma?'

'Very simple to describe, young Jacob,' said the doctor as we walked. 'The tubes to the lungs get all squeezed up and the patient can't breathe out. Nasty business. Can be fatal.'

The people at the hotel all seemed to recognise Dr Terris, and no less a person than the manager escorted us to the Broadlocks' rooms.

Their suite consisted of a little hallway, with a sort of parlour to the left and a bedroom to the right. At that time I had little knowledge of hotel rooms, but it seemed obvious from the richness of the decorations that this was a pretty expensive suite. The connecting double-doors between the two main rooms were open when I entered with the doctor. We found Broadlock in the parlour, dousing the fire in there with a carafe of water.

'Good morning, sir,' said the doctor, and shook Mr Broadlock's hand. Broadlock gazed down at the man (Dr Terris was a little on the short side) with a look of deep concern.

'A case of asthma, my young friend tells me?' Dr Terris began. 'Very wise to get rid of the fire, if such is really the case. Coal-dust, of course. Not good for the pipes.'

I could see Mrs Broadlock lying like a dead woman on the hotel bed. There was steam rising from the recently-doused bedroom fire. Apart from the loud sound of Mrs Broadlock's breathing, there was no other sign of life in the room. The coarse noise she made didn't seem to fit with the appearance of such a delicate young woman. As we proceeded into the bedroom, I got my first proper look at the sick woman's face. I realised that my old benefactor had married a woman who was perhaps half his age.

'Mrs Broadlock,' said the doctor, leaning over her. She moved her pale blue eyes to the dapper little man. 'Good. I see that you can hear me. I'm Doctor Terris of Durham. I'm just going to listen to your chest and see how we can make you a little more comfortable.' He turned to Mr Broadlock and myself, and we both went through the double doors into the other room.

The doctor closed the doors quietly and, I would say, ceremoniously. Broadlock threw himself onto an easy chair in the corner and covered his eyes with his hand. I stood near the outer door. A few minutes later we heard a knock. It was the hotel manager with a maid who had brought soap, a fresh white towel and a jug and bowl with warm water.

Right on cue, Dr Terris reappeared, smiling, and washed his hands in the bowl while the maid held it. She curtseyed awkwardly, trying not to spill the water, and withdrew with the manager when he had finished. Mr Broadlock stood up.

'What do you think, Doctor?' he asked, a map of worry sketched out on his face.

'Well,' he said in a low voice, 'she certainly does have asthma, and I'd say she's in the middle of an acute attack.' He looked round to check that the double-doors were properly closed. 'It might have been caused by the inconvenience attending the train journey, or the smoke and smuts from the locomotive. The colder weather up here might also have been a factor. I believe you've come all the way up from Croydon?' Broadlock nodded.

The doctor continued. 'She may be overly excited about travelling so far north. In any case, we can relieve her symptoms immediately. Young Jacob will return momentarily with this prescription.' The doctor handed me a sheet of paper and, bowing to Mr Broadlock, left the room as I did. He seemed to know the labyrinthine corridors of the hotel as if he'd lived there as a child. He had no doubt attended to many patients who had become sick in those luxurious surroundings.

The doctor took the opportunity to talk to me about something other than young Mrs Broadlock.

'You will understand that I have broken off relations with my son since he started to live with that Yankee charlatan fellow?' he asked, as we went down the hotel's massive oak stairs. His cheeks glowed with angry red dots as he said this.

'Of course,' I said.

'I am nevertheless Allan's father, and I'm still concerned about him. I know that you are his friend. How is he?'

'On the whole, I think you would be pleased with his progress. He seems to have given up drink altogether, and he says the pain in his hand is gone.' We left the hotel, crossed the road together and entered the pharmacy. Dr Terris and I continued to talk in a confidential tone while the pharmacist went into the back to make up the prescription.

'I expected him to come home to ask for money,' said the doctor. 'But he has not done so. I cut off his allowance, you know.'

'I think Esau Harrison is providing for him, and of course he's living at Harrison's lodgings and eating most of his meals there. He works as Harrison's assistant.'

'Yes,' the doctor said, grimly. 'I've wanted Tiger to take up some kind of occupation for years. But I did not envisage his becoming secretary to a witch-doctor. Perhaps this Harrison takes a sort of satisfaction from beguiling the son of a man of science with a heap of mumbo-jumbo. Allan still comes to see you?'

'Oh yes,' I said, although the frequency of Tiger's visits had been dwindling of late.

'I'd be very much obliged if you could inform me of any adverse change in his life. He is an only child, you know. And now he's living with that devil. That devil, I say.' Dr Terris seemed quite put out, and was obliged to blow his nose.

'I understand Harrison has brought off some

remarkable cures,' I said, growing impatient at the slowness of the pharmacist.

'He's a faith-healer. Such people can only cure people who are not really ill. I'd love to see that bearded lunatic cure a pitman with a fractured skull!'

'It's hypnotism he uses, isn't it?' I asked.

'Oh yes, and they say some hypnotists can even cure asthma, but Mr Robson and I don't believe that, do we?' Terris's remark was addressed to the pharmacist, who had now reappeared at his counter.

'Trust to drugs,' said the pharmacist, who was not, by the way, the same man Harrison had attacked. 'They're tried and tested, and they're scientific. And many of them, they're natural, aren't they doctor?'

'Indeed, Mr Robson. Why, most of the useful drugs Mr Robson has here are drawn from simple plants that grow by the wayside.' I took a bottle wrapped in a brown paper bag from the pharmacist, and bade Dr Terris a good morning.

You may imagine that I tore across the road and up the hotel stairs with the prescription, which turned out to be an evil-looking fluid in a stoppered flask. The instructions stated that the patient was to drink a dessert-spoon full, and no more, twice a day. With his knowledge of Latin,

Mr Broadlock was able to make sense of the rest of the label on the flask. 'This is Belladonna,' he said, as he stood in the living-room of the apartment.

'Belladonna? That's deadly nightshade, isn't it? It's poisonous.'

'She's had it before, very often, and in this exact dosage,' he said mournfully. 'It's supposed to relax the bronchial tubes. It used to work very well on her, but its effectiveness is diminishing. Minnie's constitution is so delicate, the doctors dare not increase the dose.'

He sent me down to the hotel restaurant for a dessert-spoon, and when he had it he vanished behind the double-doors with the flask. I heard his voice and, for the first time, hers, although I could not make out what they were saying. He reappeared and said, 'Please don't feel obliged to stay, Jacob, but if you have no other business, I'd appreciate some company during the wait.'

'The wait?'

'To see if the medicine works. We should know in about an hour.'

Mr Broadlock sent down for coffee and sandwiches. I was hungry and ate half of them in about a minute, a culinary feat that I would be very ill-advised to attempt today. Not being used to coffee in those days, I made myself a very tepid and milky cup. Mr Broadlock ate none of the sandwiches and merely sipped at a half-cup of black, unsweetened coffee. Between sips, he stared at the door to the bedroom.

I could tell he was listening for any sounds from that direction, but there were none. I assumed that we were not in the sickroom itself, either because it would have been indelicate for me to be there, or because we might waste the sick woman's air. Or perhaps my friend believed in the old proverb about a watched kettle never coming to the boil.

At last he put down his coffee, took out his pocket-watch and looked at me. He put the watch away.

'I met her down at Margate,' he said, in answer to a question that I had certainly not posed. 'She's the daughter of an old college friend of mine. He had moved down to Margate from Sanderstead, because of Minnie's asthma.'

'Did it help?' I asked.

'I think so. Anyway, I used to take my dear Mother down to Margate to stay with them every year in the summer. When I was a young man, Minnie was just a child, of course. But after Mother died, Minnie became more and more dear to me.'

'What about Minnie's mother?' I asked.

'Her mother had died giving birth to Minnie.

49

Minnie was her first and only child. When her father, my friend, also died, the question arose of what was to happen to my darling girl. As you can see, I stepped in and claimed my prize.'
I nodded and smiled.

So this was the courtship of the eminent QC, now evolved into a judge. He had waited until most people would say it was too late for him to marry at all, and then he married a girl who had known him as a sort of unofficial uncle of her childhood. Having spent years looking after his ailing mother, he now had the responsibility of looking after an ailing wife. It sounded as if he had not even *courted* his wife in the usual way, but rather *caught* her, as she was about to fall into a prolonged spinsterhood, following her father's death.

Thinking of the bundle of delicate bones in the hotel bedroom, I mentally pictured my own dear Hebe with a spark of pride. In those days she was a broad-shouldered, deep-chested girl with a loud laugh. She could bound up the stairs from our kitchen in the cellar carrying a heavy pot of stew or a pile of dinner-plates, with no more effect on her person than an enhanced rosiness in her cheeks.

After an hour, Mr Broadlock stole into the bedroom of his hotel suite, leaving the door wide open. He beckoned me to follow him. The rasping noise of Minnie's breathing not improved at all, as far as I could tell. Her eyes were open, although I suspected that she was near sleep. The pupils of her eyes were hideously dilated by the belladonna, so that they seemed like the glass eyes of a china doll.

Chapter V

Very early the next morning, I was woken by rain. My wife, as usual, slept soundly beside me while our bedroom was filled with rattlings and gurgling noises. My first action was to slide our (empty) chamber-pot from under the bed and to place it under one of our perennial, indefatigable and irreparable leaks. We lived, in effect, in a medieval house, and I suspected that some of the leaks were centuries old.

I pushed the curtains apart and gazed down into the street. Down below, Elvet Bridge had become a veritable river, lit up by the gas street-lamps that then adorned it. I suspected that the real river below the bridge would be rising up its banks, scouring earth out of the roots of trees and depositing it by the cartload on the riverside paths. Our own cellar was built into the top of the bridge, and it had not flooded in living memory. But I felt sorry for the shopkeepers nearer the water, whose stock might soon be spoiled.

I was rather pleased to have been woken by the rain, even though I now had to go around in my nightshirt and place buckets under five different leaks. I had been dreaming an unpleasant dream about Minnie Broadlock. I dreamed that she was suffocating in her luxurious hotel room, and reaching out her arms to me to save her. When I returned to bed that night, I found myself hoping that the damp atmosphere brought by the rain might help poor Minnie's breathing in some way.

The following morning, the rain had stopped but the streets were still wet. Small knots of early shoppers, washerwomen and delivery boys were standing on the bridges of the city, admiring the swollen brown river. I had business in Claypath again and my eye caught on a crowd of people in the middle of the market-place. In the midst of the delighted crown was a man with a small elephant.

I was surprised to see such a sight in Durham, and wondered if I might still be asleep and dreaming. Both the *mahout* and his charge were painted with brown mud up to their knees. The man was a black man, with a tobacco-stained fringe of otherwise white beard around his face, but with no moustache. For the most part, he wore the clothes of a normal English workman in winter, and even had his trousers tied with strings under the knee. His dirty yellow bowler hat and red neckerchief did, however, mark him out as one of the 'showfolks', as they say in the Durham dialect.

He was giving out handbills for the circus. As the son of a printer, I was able to see that, though the adult elephant at the centre of the sheet had been well drawn, the whole thing had been badly printed on something akin to a very thin grey sugar-paper. The writing under the elephant on the sheet promised:

'*Elephants, Lions, Tigers, Acrobatic Horses, Maximus the Fire-Eater, The Beautiful Bearded Lady, The Wild Man of Tasmania, The Greatest Juggler in the World and Herbert the Human Giraffe. Truly an entertaining, edifying and most educational presentation.*'

The bottom of the sheet had been irregularly cut off with a sharp knife, or something of the sort.

'That's been scissored off, y'see. That's where the dates of our engagements were,' said the *mahout* to a lady nearby. 'We don't know what dates we'll be playing at the moment,' he went on. 'As soon as we got to Ox's Meadow, the heavens opened. It rained heavy, right through the night, and now it's just a big barrel of mud down there. The council'll 'ave to let us have a few more days. We can't play till it's all dried out, and we can't go to the next engagement till we've dug out the caravans. They've sunk in, y'see.'

My friend the reverend doctor Considine was standing near the elephant. From his gaiters and wide-awake hat, and from the hand-lens he wore on a thin chain round his neck, it was pretty obvious to everyone that he was one of those enthusiastic Gilbert White-ing clergymen. He asked, of the *mahout*, 'I suppose that where you come from, it's pretty parched most of the time, eh?'

'Not really, yer 'onour,' said the black man, failing to hit on the correct term of address.

'Where *do* you come from then?' asked the man of the cloth, clearly puzzled.

'Liverpool, yer 'onour,' the black man replied, and raised a laugh from the spectators.

Considine looked momentarily stunned, but recovered sufficiently to walk away in the direction of the Cathedral. It was clear that, though his knowledge of Gilbert White and Darwin, and of the local flora and fauna, may have been comprehensive, his knowledge of the provenances of some members of the human species was incomplete.

Not before time, I realised the elephant and his handler might make a good photograph. I paid the man sixpence to stay there for a few minutes, and went rapidly out of the Market

Place and over Elvet Bridge. In the studio, I slipped a plate into the more portable of our two cameras, and hurried with the camera and its heavy wooden tripod to the market-place.

I then took the best picture of my whole photographic career. It was a dull morning and the exposure had to be long. Luckily, both *mahout* and elephant remained quite still, and everything was in focus. I think I have sold thousands of prints of that picture over the years, mostly in the form of souvenir postcards. The picture includes part of St Nicholas's Church, and I called it 'The Varieties of God's Creation.' Many people in Durham still have framed enlargements of the picture on their walls at home.

When I had taken the picture, I gave the man another sixpence. I put the tripod over my left shoulder and the camera under my right arm. On my way up Claypath to Gilesgate, I couldn't resist a left turn down Providence Row to Ox's Meadow. This was where all of the circuses visiting Durham pitched their tents. The circus encampment was a scene of apparent chaos, which, if viewed properly, had a good deal of order in it. Every likely tree, bush, fence or post had been pressed into service as a drying rack, or the fastening-place for a guy-rope. The guy-ropes of the tents were being used as washing-lines, and a system for recovering sunken objects, rather like that of a bucket-line, was in operation.

Some of the show-folks were picking through their flood-soaked gear, looking for anything that had been stained with mud. The children then took this stuff down to the river where a team of women rinsed it out. Eventually it all ended up on a guy-rope, a bush or a fence.

The only people not engaged in washing were some men digging out a caravan that had sunk up to its axles in mud. One of these men, an enormous fellow stripped to the waist, was evidently the circus strongman. A group of rather well-to-do married ladies stood beside me on the road, obviously admiring this pipe-smoking Hercules.

The diggers were nearing the end of their task, and an adult elephant was being put into an improvised yoke to help pull the caravan out. I thought about trying to take a picture, but the men looked too busy to stand still and be photographed. In any case, to get anything other than a general view, I would have had to march through many yards of sucking mud, with the camera under my arm.

That afternoon, leaving the plate exposed with the elephant picture in a lightproof box, I visited Mr Esau Harrison. I had two good reasons to do so. Dr Terris had charged me with the task of discreetly watching over my old friend Tiger. If at all possible, I also wished to consult with the American about the case of Minnie Broadlock, who seemed not to be responding to Dr Terris's treatment at all.

I knocked on the door and was shown in by the landlady, who occupied most of the ground floor of this high-class lodging house. Harrison's door, on the first floor, was opened by a clean-shaven young man I did not recognise, wearing a hat and a checked suit that seemed oddly familiar.

'Would it be possible to have a few words with Mr Harrison?' I asked. The young fellow grinned back at me in a very familiar way.

'Don't you recognise me, Blount?' he asked, his voice rather subdued. Of course, the sound of his voice clinched it. 'Tiger?' I asked, incredulous.

'Not Tiger any more,' he said, his finger at his lips to suggest quietness. 'You'll have to call me Allan now.'

'But what have you done to yourself?' I whispered.

'Been to the barber's, old chap,' he said. 'Dumped the old whiskers.'

'It makes you look younger,' I said. I did not mention that he now looked as if his head were much too small for his body.

He showed me in, this disconcerting semi-stranger, and I noticed at once the coldness of the flat. I had taken my hat off, but immediately wished I had kept it on, as my Quaker forebears on my mother's side would have done. It was raining thinly outside and the dampness of the atmosphere had made this another unusually cold day. I think it was actually colder in Harrison's flat that it was in the street.

'The boss doesn't hold with heating a room,' said Tiger, or rather Allan, noticing how I had folded my arms against the cold. 'He doesn't like gaslight, either. Says it heats the room up too much, and the residue is bad for the lungs. Never eats hot food, and as you've probably noticed, always wears thin clothes, whatever the season. Only takes cold showers, as well. But he doesn't mind me wearing this thick old suit, and Adah dresses up warm. She often wears that red beret indoors.'

We were in a large sitting-room, which I judged to have been newly papered and furnished. In most rooms of this type, the chairs seem to naturally point themselves at the fire. Since this fire was never used, the chairs had turned themselves to face the window, through which I caught a glimpse of the building-site that was soon to become the magnificent glazed-brick edifice of the Shire Hall.

'Do you sleep in this flat every night?' I asked my friend.

'Oh yes. I'm really part of the family now. I sleep in that bedroom to your right'.

'The flat is pretty nice, isn't it?' I remarked.

'I suppose it is, yes.'

'I mean, Mr Harrison must pay a lot of money for it, per month?'

'I suppose so. I've never thought about it...'

'So where does he *get* his money, this Esau Harrison?'

'Oh, from wealthy people he's cured, of course. And he accepts contributions from his followers here in Durham. We saw some of them at the theatre, do you remember? Many of them are widows 'richly left' as they say.' Allan had misapplied a phrase from Shakespeare's *Merchant of Venice*. I noticed that my friend was leaning close to me and whispering as we spoke. From this I inferred that someone else was in the flat with us.

'Is Mr Harrison out?' I asked.

'No no. He always has a nap after lunch. It's the only meal he eats, you know. No breakfast or dinner for him. He's in the larger of the two bedrooms.'

'Trying to digest one of Mrs Roberson's pork chops, eh?' I asked, naming the landlady.

'Oh no! That would be hot food. And anyway, Esau is a vegetarian. He ate a large salad for lunch today.' I stared at Allan open-mouthed. What would Mrs Roberson think of this lodger, who didn't use her gas or coals, and didn't want her to cook for him, or even to give him cold meat?

'When does Mr Harrison finish his little *siesta* ?' I asked.

'At two o'clock precisely every day,' said my friend, looking at the clock on the mantelpiece. It showed seven minutes past two. Allan looked at the clock and checked it against his own pocket-watch. He looked puzzled.

'Do you think he'll agree to see me when he wakes up?' I asked.

'I don't know, but it's very unusual for him to oversleep. Why do you want to talk to him?'

'I just want to ask him some questions about a medical case. Does he have an alarm clock? Perhaps somebody forgot to wind it up.'

'He doesn't use an alarm clock. He just wakes at precisely the right time.' Allan rose, in some agitation, and knocked on the bedroom door. His answer was a long, deep groan from within. 'You'd better stay there,' Allan instructed me. 'I'll see what's wrong.'

The door was not locked. Allan slipped through it very quickly, but I caught a brief, shocking glance of the famous Mr Esau Harrison. He was wearing his familiar fawn suit. He was kneeling in the middle of the bed, his head towards its head. His back was horizontal and his hands clasped the iron backrest. He was rocking backwards and forwards slightly and there was a faint squeaking coming from the bed-frame.

I heard nothing for a while after the door closed, and I briefly considered leaving the flat, so as not to intrude.

I wandered over to the door and called, 'Allan! I can get a doctor! It doesn't have to be your father.' There was no answer.

On his new employer's home ground, Allan was being unusually off-hand with me. Thanks to the loss of his beard, he now looked like a stranger. He also seemed to be acting like a stranger to me, his best friend in the city.

I wandered around the room impatiently, and decided to distract myself by reading the spines of Esau Harrison's books. He had about a dozen of them, in various states of repair. They were arranged in a pile on top of a small occasional table. I was then, and still am, as much of a book collector as my pocket can reasonably allow. Mr Broadlock had sent me books every year for my birthday and for Christmas. These had included the works of Shakespeare, Tennyson, Milton and the American Quaker poet, Whittier. I recognised Milton's *Paradise Lost* among Harrison's books, as well as a Shakespeare's *The Tempest*. There was a volume of Hoffman's stories done into English, and something by the brothers Grimm. The rest of the books were theological in nature.

In those days, there was an odd enthusiasm for reading books that had been excluded from the Bible; the so-called apocryphal books. Harrison had several individual volumes that I took to be books of this type. He had *The Shepherd of Hermas* and *The Acts of Paul and Thecla*, both written in the Christian era. He also had *Esdras*, *Ecclesiasticus* and *The Book of Esau*. Before I could start to flick through any of these, the door was opened and Allan and Harrison entered the room.

Harrison was trying to look composed, but his indisposition had deepened and reddened the lines around his mouth and eyes. He loped to the window, using his characteristic bow-legged gait, and opened it. He sighed heavily as he sat in a low easy chair by the open window. A few drops of rain strayed onto the windowsill. Allan stood by him, as if waiting for some command. I stared at the two of them, embarrassed.

'A touch of colic, Mr Blount,' Harrison explained. 'A penalty of old age. Please sit down. Allan, please fetch a wet flannel and some water for us to drink.' Allan dodged round behind me and entered what was obviously the bathroom. Twisting my head, I saw that there was a water-tap above the bath. It looked as if Mrs Roberson's improvements to her furnished rooms had included a properly plumbed-in bath with a shower attachment, a rarity in those days. There was no hot water on tap, and I assumed that Mr Harrison, with his love of low temperatures, would never ask for any hot bath water to be brought up in jugs from Mrs Roberson's kitchen.

Harrison wiped his face with the wet flannel, and then handed it back to Allan. Eventually, my friend appeared with a carafe of water and three glasses.

'Allan, sit here by me,' said my friend's new master. 'So, Mr Blount,' he began, 'I understand you have some questions to ask me?' The two of them looked at me from either side of the window, drinking their glasses of water. I looked at the glass carafe and the remaining tumbler glistening greyly on a second occasional table. In a cold room, on a rainy day, a glass of water is not the most hospitable thing to offer to a guest.

I was stuck for a moment – unable to think of what I had to ask. I stared at the hunting prints that Mrs Roberson had caused to be put on the walls. Then I remembered poor little Mrs

Broadlock, suffering in her hotel room just along Old Elvet.

'A dear friend of mine has come up to visit me with his new wife. When I met them at the station, she was in the middle of a seizure. It seems that she suffers from asthma...'

'Asthma,' repeated Harrison, when I had explained the situation. 'As it happens, asthma is a very suitable condition for the exercise of my talents, and in fact for the demonstration of my theories. Some more conventional healers will say that different mental states can trigger it. I say that the soul is involved in such cases.'

'So you think you can cure her?' I asked. 'You must understand, Mr Broadlock is my great friend and benefactor...'

'If you had been able to hear what I had to say to that audience at the theatre, you would not have had to ask such a question. Although I believe that Allan has told you something of my approach, you were robbed of a fuller understanding by that ridiculous claque. What you have to understand is this: the cure of the body is the business of such people as Allan's learned father, the good Dr Terris. My calling is to cure the soul – the immortal part of man, and woman of course, which inhabits our bodies until death.

'My particular ability is not so widely

respected as that of Dr Terris, but it is in fact much more useful. You see, all Dr Terris's patients will die; but their souls will not. The life of the body is very short, in comparison to eternity. To have cured a case of gout will give only very short-lived comfort. Even if Dr Terris helps a gouty patient to live in comfort and be as old as Adam was when he died, the good doctor will have done little to cure his soul.'

This was all very interesting, and Harrison delivered it from his shadowy corner in his rich, compelling voice. It was not, however, an answer to the question of whether he could cure poor Minnie Broadlock. He detected my impatience, and went on: 'Asthma is one of those diseases where Dr Terris will supply an accurate diagnosis, and a prognosis, but no real cure or even an explanation of *why* the condition should occur. Why should the breathing-tubes suddenly decide to narrow themselves, to the point where the patient's life is endangered?' There was a silence.

'So, do you know why?' I asked, impressed despite myself with Harrison's knowledge of this unusual condition.

'Such symptoms as are associated with asthma occur when the soul is not in agreement with the body. Other conditions of this type would include chronic drunkenness, when the diseased soul demands the consumption of ardent spirits that the body cannot well tolerate. Gluttony is another example: the overloaded stomach cries out for the mouth to stop eating, but the soul remains hungry.'

I was beginning to be a little convinced by this, but I tried to keep my mind on the matter in hand. 'I have not spoken to Mr Broadlock about consulting with you,' I explained. 'But he obviously wants to help his wife get better. If I ask him now if it would be acceptable, could you see Mrs Broadlock tomorrow morning?'

'Of course.'

'Mr Broadlock is a wealthy man, I believe. He is in fact a judge…'

'Allan here now deals with anything to do with money,' said the American. ' If you could wait for him outside in the street, Mr Blount, your friend will join you in a moment. You should both see Mr Broadlock straight away, to see if he is agreeable to my visiting his wife.'

Outside, the light rain had gone and the sun had come out again. The afternoon seemed to me to contain the makings of a beautiful, if chilly, evening. Allan Terris quickly joined me, and we walked toward the County Hotel to see Mr Broadlock. When we were halfway there, Allan stopped and leaned against a wall.

'Mr Harrison has told me that he doesn't want money in return for treating Mrs

Broadlock.'

'So what does he want?'

'He doesn't want anything – at least he doesn't want you to feel obliged to give him anything.'

'Me? What about Mr Broadlock? He's the one who should be sent the bill.'

'There will be no bill. I am Harrison's friend, and you are my friend, and Mrs Broadlock is your friend. One does not charge one's friends for favours.'

'Actually, I've barely met Mrs Broadlock,' I explained. Allan thought for a moment. 'Mr Harrison values friendship very highly,' he said. 'As you know, he is under a slight indisposition today, but he feels sure that he will be able to attend the young lady tomorrow.'

I thought, we'll owe him a favour, myself and Mr Broadlock. And will he not expect a favour in return? If so, what favour will he ask of us, and when?

Chapter VI

At the hotel, I went up to the Broadlocks' suite with Allan. Broadlock had never heard of Harrison before, and I tried to explain that, although he claimed to be a doctor, he gave a strong impression of being something else. Broadlock agreed to let Esau Harrison see his wife, as long as he, Broadlock, could be in the room at the same time. I tried to put across something of what I understood of Harrison's theories, but Broadlock seemed too tired and desperate to listen. We arranged for Harrison to come to the hotel the next day.

Downstairs, I managed to persuade Allan to join me in the bar of the hotel. I smoked a small cigar and drank a half-pint of beer; he drank lemonade and didn't smoke anything. The bar at the County was then and is now a terribly respectable place to drink. Allan had, however, been reluctant to come in with me at all. This, I thought, is the man who, in the past, has ventured into the roughest taverns in the north of England, and kept pace with the drinking of hardened pitmen.

'Working for Mr Harrison seems to have changed you a great deal, Allan,' I observed.

'I suppose so,' he said, passing the knuckles of his right hand over his close-shaven cheek.

'You don't just eat once a day like him, do you?'

'Not yet. He doesn't want me to make that change too suddenly. At present, I am down to just breakfast and dinner. It's really surprisingly easy to cut out lunch.'

'And are you a vegetarian like him?' He shook his head slightly.

'Again, it's a gradual process. I no longer eat beef or pork. I just eat a little fish and poultry. But I mustn't eat any meat in the flat. I go to a chophouse, or the temperance restaurant.' I remembered that Tiger Terris had only recently eaten and drunk himself into a happy stupor during a Christmas feast at my uncle's house.

'And no gaspers, and no booze?' He had nothing to say to this. 'Well, if you ever get tired of it,' I went on, 'I'm sure your dad will be pleased to see you living back with him. Absence makes the heart grow fonder, you know. You'll be the Wanderer Returns, the Prodigal Son.'

'Hardly prodigal,' he said. I laughed at this,

thinking it a joke, but he didn't laugh.

We walked in silence back to his new lodgings, where he went in and I continued home, having first reminded him that he should come to my house for dinner soon. 'I'm sure Hebe can cook us up something Pythagorean,' I said, using an old word for 'vegetarian' that I had picked up somewhere.

In the short distance between Allan's diggings and the photographer's shop, I passed Adah Harrison in the street. I tipped my hat to her and bowed slightly, but she 'cut me dead' as they say. She seemed to be in a great hurry. If she too were Pythagorian, I thought, then she is a credit to her diet. In the orange, waning light her skin seemed very clear, like bone china. Her black hair, trailing out of her beret, was glossy and strong-looking. Pallor and slenderness don't always indicate poor health, I thought.

At home, Hebe asked me whether I had spoken to Esau Harrison's daughter.

'She wasn't there, but she ignored me when I saw her in the town,' I explained. We were taking dinner up from the kitchen to the parlour, which doubled as our dining room.

'I see her in the market, sometimes,' Hebe said, referring to our Durham Indoor Market. 'She looks underfed to me, you know. Looks like she could do with a nice steak and kidney

71

pie like this one.' I explained about the eccentric household that Harrison was the head of, and the frugal diet thereof.

'Vegetarianism? No alcohol? No heating? That's not what *she* wants. I know what that's all about. He's just an old miser.'

In the parlour, we put a pie, the potatoes and the green vegetables on trivets in the middle of the table. The table was set for three. Hebe poured out some sherry for both of us and proceeded to quiz me about every detail of Mrs Roberson's newly-decorated apartments. I was able to answer almost all of her questions, because after years gazing into viewfinders I had developed something of the photographer's eye for detail.

My description of Harrison's plumbed-in bath gave her pause. At that time we kept a zinc-plated bath hanging in the alley behind the building. Baths were taken in the kitchen, because otherwise the water had to be carried up two flights of stairs (we could hardly bathe in the studio, the roof of which was partly glazed). The only water-tap in our house at that time was in the kitchen, and even water required for photographic purposes had to be carried through the partition in an enamel jug. When the bath-water was finished with, I used to haul the bath over the brick floor of the kitchen and cast the dirty water into a drain in the yard.

Before Hebe had had a chance to persuade me that we should pay for a plumbed-in bath, I heard our dinner-guest on the stairs: we had left the door unlocked in expectation of his arrival.

My father-in-law, Detective Inspector Albert Maitland, was a tall, stout man with pepper-and-salt side-whiskers. He was a widower, and relied on Hebe to cook him a decent dinner whenever duty did not call him out of town.

As usual, he greeted us with a gruff 'Jacob' and a 'Hebe'. We never expected any conversation out of him until he had eaten a large dinner. Eating was his means of relaxation, and one could see from his figure that he relaxed regularly in this way. Hebe usually cooked about as much for him as she did for the both of us.

He threw his hat and coat onto our easy chair by the fire and sat down at the head of the table. He then proceeded to undo the penultimate button of his waistcoat. I took this as my cue to sit down next to him, and Hebe took it as her cue to begin to serve dinner. As Hebe started to serve me, her father started to pitch in. When he was helping himself to seconds, Hebe and I were only halfway through our first helpings. On a very good day, when I was very hungry to start with, I could finish my normal-sized dinner by the time my father-in-law had finished his two portions.

Maitland had started life as a miner. In this profession he had gained a reputation as a prodigious worker, eater, drinker and fighter. His reputation as a hard man did him no harm in his police career. Tight-lipped witnesses tended to tell all, once Maitland started to question them. Criminals liable to resist arrest would not do so if they knew that Maitland's hand was feeling their collar. This saved him a lot of time and brought him some celebrated arrests. He had gone rapidly into private-clothes work, risen rapidly through the ranks and stopped at Detective Inspector.

On the evening of the day when I first visited Esau Harrison, Maitland finished his dinner before us, as usual, and began to turn his attention to the two bottles of wine he had brought with him. Once he was sure that Hebe and myself had a glass each, he felt that the rest was his rightful share. As he finished the first bottle, he started to be affable and talkative, and undid the remaining buttons of his waistcoat. I decided to ask him if any notable crimes had happened in the city that day.

'Theft of an 'am,' he said, looking at me with one eye closed.

'Theft of a what, father?' Hebe asked.

'A ham,' he said, 'down by the river.'

'But what are the circumstances surrounding this evil deed?'

'Shakespeare was to blame,' he said.

'Shakespeare? Was he not somewhat hindered by the fact that he has been dead and buried for nearly three hundred years?'

'You forget, my son-in-law,' he explained. 'Shakespeare the man may be dead, but his works live on.'

'Ah, so the ham was stolen by a play?'

My father-in-law took another drink, then he told us the story.

'There was a bunch of them Pareesians 'avin' a picnic down by the river...'

'Parisians, father?' Hebe asked.

'Yes, you know. They're not really French or anything. They just wear French clothes and look stupid. They're the pathetics or something.'

'The Aesthetics, I think it is,' I put in. I knew the group my father-in-law was referring to. They were students, all male of course at that date, who dressed rather flamboyantly and dashed off to Paris in the college vacations. Several of them had paid me to photograph them, sometimes in the bizarre, loose, androgynous clothes of the Dress Reform Society. They smoked their cigarettes in amber holders, and eschewed beards, moustaches and whiskers. Such delicate flowers seemed somewhat out of place in the harsh northern climate of Durham.

The University authorities were uneasy about the Parisians, but they were all 'brilliant' academically (as they said about themselves) and on the whole probably did less harm than the whiskery, hard-drinking students who fought pitched battles with the town lads up and down the city every Friday night.

'Two of these Parisian boys were doin' a bit from *A Midsummer Night's Dream* in front of the Count's House. Everyone was looking at them of course, and away from the river. That was when the ham went missing.'

I should explain, for the benefit of readers who don't know Durham, that the Count's House, so called, is not really a house at all. It is a folly, in the form of a little picturesque Grecian temple, which once decorated the garden of a Polish count who lived near the river. When the riverside walks were made, the Count's House found itself marooned on the edge of a public pathway. The reason why some people think the Count might have lived there is because the Count was in fact a dwarf.

A winter picnic with theatricals by the river sounded like a lot of fun. I assumed that the 'Parisians' would have been knocking back brandy or absinthe to keep out the cold.

'What bit from *Midsummer Night's Dream* were they doing, father-in-law?' I asked the Inspector.

'*Ill met by moonlight*, one of them said.'

'But that's a scene between the King and Queen of the fairies,' said Hebe. 'One of the boys would have had to play the Queen!'

I asked one last question. 'Maitland, if they were performing as you say, the King and Queen of the fairies would have been facing the river. They might have seen the robbery.'

'I thought of that,' Maitland replied, belatedly congratulating himself with another glass of wine. 'The King of the Fairies didn't see anything – he was showing off his fine profile to the spectators, apparently. And the Queen, well he, she, is short-sighted. He's called Andrew Sekt. He doesn't like to wear his glasses because those Parisians don't like the look of them. He could make out very little, but what he thought he saw was an ape – like a big gorilla – coming half out of the river, then going back again.' There was a brief pause and I said, 'He must be very short-sighted I suppose.'

'I think so,' Hebe put in. 'I mean, we don't have gorillas in England do we?'

'No,' I said. 'And I don't think they can swim, anyway.'

'So, Mr Maitland,' I said, 'I hope you will be dedicating the entire resources of the Durham police to finding the ham, dead or alive?'

Maitland proceeded to tell us the rest of the news in the city.

'The circus has gone, you know.'

'Really?' Hebe was disappointed.

'They said it was too muddy to open this week, and the council wouldn't let them stay for another week. They set off about lunchtime. Of course, we had to put on some constables to escort them out of the city. That's how I know. They made a sorry sight, apparently, the show people, all covered in mud.'

Chapter VII

After Maitland had gone, I helped Hebe get the plates, glasses and cutlery downstairs to the kitchen. As usual, she boiled up a kettle and made a start on the washing-up. While she clattered about at the sink, I went through into the darkroom and lit the gaslight. As often happened, I conducted a conversation with my wife over the plywood partition.

'What are you doing in there?' she asked. 'Isn't it too light to print anything?' Soon, I thought, Hebe would know the photography business as well as I did.

'Of course,' I said. 'I'm just looking through the boxes.' These were ordinary cardboard boxes containing carefully wrapped negatives, sample prints and names and addresses of subjects. I was looking through the box marked 'PORTRAITS: STUDENTS' and came upon 'SEKT: ANDREW'.

We had two portraits of the Queen of the Fairies, the negatives waiting in storage for him to request further prints. One portrait had been taken by my uncle Eadweard when Sekt had been a 'fresher' or beginner at the University. He was then a pimply youth in oval, steel-framed spectacles and a wispy attempt at side-whiskers. He was wearing a stiff high collar, a tie in a tight four-in-hand knot and a very puritanical looking frock-coat with fabric-covered buttons. In the second picture, taken by myself, the boy presented an astounding contrast to his former self. He had cast off his spectacles and shaved off his whiskers. The collar was soft and bohemian, the tie patterned with strange swirling shapes. The jacket was lighter, both in colour and weight, and very sharp-looking. This change was evidently all to do with the influence of his connection with the Parisians, or Aesthetics.

I showed the two pictures to Hebe. She was also very struck by the contrast. 'Those glasses don't look very strong,' she said. She was right. Strong glasses distort the appearance of the eyes, making them look either larger or smaller. There was little distortion to be seen in the earlier picture. I checked that young Sekt's college address had been kept with his likenesses.

The following morning, I met Mr Broadlock in the foyer of the County Hotel. Mr Harrison was a little late, and I had time to observe that Mr Broadlock's own condition had deteriorated even since the last time I had seen him. He was drinking a half-pint of stout, though it was only about nine o'clock in the morning. I hardly needed to ask him if Minnie was still unwell, or how he felt about unleashing this strange American hypnotist on her.

When Harrison arrived, he was arm-in-arm with both Allan Terris and Adah Harrison. From a distance, it looked as if they might be walking in this way out of a feeling of mutual affection. Close up, it was pretty clear that his two companions were actually supporting Esau Harrison. Since a lady was approaching, Broadlock and myself stood up.

Harrison eased himself into an armchair and put his cane across the arms. He was sitting just to my left, and I was able to observe the head of the cane as he twisted it around. The head was made of ivory, of the brown, striated sort I recognised as ancient mammoth ivory. It had been carved into the shape of miniature wolf's head. Looking up at Harrison himself, his face seemed to me almost as pale and shiny as ivory from a modern elephant. He was gripping the shaft of the cane so hard that his knuckles were turning white. With his hands in this position, he looked as if he were holding onto a ship's railing in a storm at sea.

Soon after Harrison was seated, Adah excused herself, saying that she was going shopping. As she departed, we all sat down on chairs arranged in a square, with a low onyx-topped table between us. One of the hotel waiters appeared at Broadlock's shoulder, but he angrily sent him away. He assumed his professional persona of a lawyer now, and without any small-talk, started negotiations.

'Mr Harrison, I understand from this young man that you have some expertise as a healer of sorts?' Harrison looked at him, but did not respond with word, gesture or expression. Broadlock went on, 'I would not normally engage the services of a healer without any conventional medical qualifications. My wife's asthma has, however, proved intractable. Dr Terris thinks that she is in grave danger. I will pay you five pounds, in advance, and you may keep it whether you cure her or not.'

'I do not want any payment, Mr Broadlock,' Harrison explained, in a low, cracked voice. 'And if you have been told that I am not a fully-qualified doctor in the so-called 'scientific' branch of medicine, then you have been misinformed.' This went some way to disarming Broadlock, but he still snapped up out of his chair and stood with a very straight back, like a soldier. 'I must be in the room for the whole time you are with Minnie,' he said.

'Of course,' Harrison replied, pushing himself out of his own chair by bearing down on the top of his cane. 'You are fighting against your scepticism about me, are you not?' he asked Broadlock. 'Have you been asking the hotel staff about my activities in this city?'. This gave Broadlock pause.

'I have heard that Anton Mesmer, a physician of Vienna, achieved some remarkable cures by hypnotism,' said Broadlock. 'I think Mesmer may have been the victim of some political wrangling when he appeared to succumb to the supposed evidence against him.'

'He certainly had his enemies,' said the American. 'All men who have followers also inevitably have enemies. You understand, though, that in my case Mesmerism is not an end in itself. It is just a tool. The real healing is to do with the soul.' I wondered whether this was really just a theory of his, or whether it had become his *idée fixe*.

'This is a Christian country, sir,' Broadlock asserted. 'I think that most of us believe in the soul. It is the means by which we connect ourselves to eternity.' Harrison grunted assent. I suspected that his idea of the soul had very little to do with churches and ministers.

Allan and myself stood up, and we all made our way to the stairs. Harrison proceeded rather slowly, making much use of his wolf-headed stick.

In the Broadlocks' suite, Minnie appeared to be about the same as when I had last seen her. Her eyes were half-open, and her breath was making that mechanical, pneumatic noise that was now becoming too familiar to me. Allan and myself stood by the door into the sitting room, while Broadlock stood at the foot of the bed. 'This is the healer we spoke of, Minnie,' he said.

Esau Harrison knelt down on the floor, on the far side of the bed, and put his head near the lady's. She acknowledged his presence with a sideways flick of her eyes. She pushed behind her with her hands, and her body seemed to creep up the bed, as if avoiding him, but he continued to stare into her face. Broadlock straightened himself and looked ready to snap Harrison's neck if he should touch even the edge of Minnie's nightgown. Harrison was smiling, slightly, obscurely, under his beard. He seemed to cast a shadow all around himself. The sight was disturbing. It is not usual for a stranger, a foreigner whose antecedents are not known to anyone, to find himself near a young English lady in her nightdress. Harrison might have been some wicked seducer, like the fiend in Bram Stoker's book, which was published around this time.

It may have been that the traffic in the street

below just happened to be very quiet at that moment, but it seemed to me that an oppressive silence emanated from Harrison when he was gazing at Minnie Broadlock. It was as if the world was a river full of noise, and he had quieted it by being a great post jutting out of the water. As the current of the river caressed him, he effortlessly gave off ripples. The ripples stilled the water slightly. The simile seems very apt to me – such posts are usually the slimy old remains of something bigger that was once there: perhaps a jetty. And a post standing up in a river can be, for the most part, concealed. We only see the top.

Harrison was gazing at Minnie with a look of puzzled fascination. He might have been trying to read her like a letter scrawled by a careless schoolgirl. When he spoke to Minnie at last, he spoke in a very quiet voice, but there had been silence for so long that the sound made me jump. His speech comprised a question, and a surprising one.

'What do you fear, Minnie?' he asked. She closed her eyes. She did not turn away from him: he already seemed to have gained her trust. 'What do you fear, Minnie?' he asked again. She gazed at him, as if fascinated. Her eyes were wider than I had ever seen them.

'What does this mean, Harrison?' Broadlock asked, breaking the spell. As if this were a cue or signal, Esau Harrison stood up. He turned to Broadlock and spoke to him as if Allan and myself were not in the room. 'It is most necessary that she answer this question, but regrettably she cannot do it now that you have interrupted us.' Harrison said this kindly, with a generous smile. He implied that it was somehow not Broadlock's fault that he had cut in. He shook Broadlock's hand and, with a gesture to Allan to follow, left the room. Broadlock rushed out into the corridor. 'Is that all?' he cried.

'By no means,' said Harrison, without turning round. Arms locked together, Allan and Harrison started down the stairs at the end of the corridor.

'A charlatan,' said Broadlock, but not until I was with him alone in the little ante-room to his suite. 'I'll not let *him* in here again!'

'I'm sorry,' I said.

'Don't blame yourself, Jacob,' he said, patting my shoulder. 'If anyone's to blame, it's your friend Allan and myself. Allan seems to have an irrational faith in the man, and I'm so desperate that I'll try anything. But no more quacks! It's Dr Terris or nobody.'

As I bade farewell to Mr Broadlock, I resolved not to do whatever favour it was that Harrison would beg of me, in return for his services. It seemed to me that he had done little or nothing for Minnie Broadlock.

Chapter VIII

As I made my way home in the mid-morning, I found myself gazing at some pretty meat pies in the window of a butcher's shop. I was a little peckish, and hoped that Hebe had procured something similar for our lunch at home. Above and behind the pies, I saw a dark, slender shape that I recognised. It was Adah Harrison. I smiled and waved, but she was sideways on to me and didn't seem to see me. I realised that I probably looked a little silly smiling and waving into the window of a butcher's shop, so I stuffed my thumbs in my waistcoat-pockets and came away. It was only when I was at home, setting up my equipment for a portrait, that it occurred to me that, strictly speaking, Adah Harrison had absolutely no reason to be in a butcher's shop. She and Esau were, after all, supposed to be vegetarians. All of their food, moreover, was supposed to be supplied by their landlady, Mrs Roberson.

Soon, an explanation came to me. Although

Esau was a vegetarian, Adah still hankered after the taste of animal flesh. She bought Mr Everall's excellent pies to enjoy as a guilty pleasure; forbidden fruit.

The portrait I was to take that morning was of the distinguished plumber of Durham, Mr Robert Bax. Bax had worked his way up from the lowly position of a plumber's apprentice to be the man relied on by all the Durham gentry to solve their plumbing problems for them. He had plumbed in our kitchen tap at cost since, as he said, 'We are fellow members of the Chemical Club of Durham.'

Bax had made a fortune from installing plumbed-in baths, washbasins and WCs in many of the new houses beyond the city's viaduct. And he had discreetly inserted pipes and drains into numerous picturesque old buildings in the older part of town. He wore a large gold 'gypsy' ring (that is, a ring designed to go on his little finger) and he didn't personally touch the baser metals of copper or lead any more. An army of some thirty workmen sprang to their tools at his command, and travelled even as far as Darlington and Newcastle, on the train, to patch up breached pipes.

Mr Bax was a good subject for a photograph, and he seemed to know it. With a tall silk hat over his bald patch, his clean-shaven face looked youthful and jolly. Although (as the hat will suggest) he was in his best morning suit, I managed to introduce a little informality into the photograph, which I took using a whole plate, as befitted his wealth and status. I persuaded Bax to look as if he was fiddling with his ring.

When I had bidden the Golden Plumber adieu, I took the exposed plate out of the camera and carefully put it in a drawer, next to my picture of the elephant. I would develop it as soon as night came. I hastily took some lunch and then proceeded to the Castle.

Durham Castle was built on the pile of earth dug out for the foundations of the Cathedral. The Norman conquerors built it to protect their friends and to keep out their enemies. Those friends who could not fit into the castle, safe atop its artificial hill, had to make do with the Cathedral. The two buildings share the top of the high, flat-topped rock, ringed with the river Wear, that dominates the centre of Durham.

When the University came to Durham, someone had the idea of using the castle as a hall of residence. Unfortunately, although the battlements had kept out the marauding Scots, they cannot keep out the various forms of idleness that are enemies to students.

As I passed through the gate into the castle I

told the porter that I would be visiting Andrew Sekt. The porter cast up his eyes and said to me, 'I 'ope you don't expect to be paid straight away.' From my clothes, he had obviously judged that I was some sort of tradesman, and had made a guess, no doubt based on experience, that I was also a creditor.

Andrew Sekt was 'sporting his wood' when I arrived; that is to say, he had closed both the inner and outer doors to his rooms. Students 'sporting the wood' in this way are meant to be hard at study, and not supposed to be disturbed. He responded to my knock, however, and I had my first look into a student's room in the University.

It was a nice large room, which looked as if it had recently been fitted out with new furniture and curtains in the 'Aesthetic' style. There was a fine Turkey carpet lying on the flags, and a small bronze of a male nude on the desk. It was tempting to conclude that Sekt's problems with creditors had something to do with the improvements to his room. It seemed to me to be a strange way for a student to waste his money. Surely drink, women and gambling were the more traditional ways for students to bankrupt themselves?

Sekt greeted me tieless, his shirt open. He wore a grey silk dressing gown over his waistcoat and smoked a cigarette in an amber holder. There was a strange tenseness visible between his eyebrows. This was the kind of thing I always had to try and notice, and eliminate, before making a photographic portrait in my studio. Other details that I had trained myself to notice included specks of food caught in beards, white lint on dark jackets, and crooked partings through hair.

When I had reminded him that I was the photographer on Elvet Bridge, I asked him about what he had seen during the picnic. I told him I wanted to photograph the beast he had seen, if possible (at that time I believed that it must be some exotic animal that had escaped from a zoo). Luckily, Sekt seemed to be in the right mood to answer my questions.

'As I told Inspector Maitland, I didn't have my glasses on, so I couldn't see anything clearly. I just saw a large, hairy form, roughly shaped like a man. It emerged from the water, came onto the bank, and then went back into the water. It's supposed to have stolen the ham, but I didn't see that part.'

'Why not?' I asked. Sekt lay down and lounged on his bed.

'When it came onto the bank, it went into some shade. There's lots of big trees hanging down near the Count's House. They're quite shady, even in winter. Anyway, when something's in shade, I can't see it so well. I see

92

better in bright sunlight.'

'I see. Well, I suppose we all do.' I looked around his room again. I tried not to look at the little male nude, which I found to be a rather embarrassing presence. 'I wonder,' I said, 'could I have a look at your glasses?'

'You can have them if you like,' he said. 'Although on second thoughts Papa is coming soon. He'll want to see me wearing them like a good little boy.' He pronounced 'Papa' in the continental way, with the stress on the first syllable. He fished his glasses out of the pocket of a jacket in the cupboard. With his permission, I put them on and looked out of his window, over to the Cathedral.

Everything looked normal at first, except that whatever I saw near the edge of the glasses looked rather pinched. Then I started to feel slightly queasy: the lenses of my eyes were adjusting to the prescription. I handed the glasses back to Sekt, who slipped them on, almost as a reflex. The tense look between his eyebrows relaxed and he looked around the room, as if for the first time.

'I don't think they're very strong,' I said. 'If you say you saw a big hairy ape at that distance when you weren't wearing them, then I think you must really have seen something like that. What I don't understand is why you carried on the performance of Shakespeare?' He laughed a little at this.

'I take my artistic activities very seriously, Mr Blount,' he said. 'I was too wrapped up in my part to break off.' Wrapped up in his part, I thought. Perhaps he had seen a kind of hallucination of Bottom, the monstrous chimera Titania sees in *A Midsummer Night's Dream*. 'Do you have any theories as to what this thing was, or is, Mr Sekt?'

'Well, I suppose the most prosaic explanation would be that it was some sort of ape escaped from a menagerie. But I choose not to be prosaic. No. I will draw on my continental origins (you will tell from my name that I am not entirely English). I will recall my dear Papa's fireside stories, and propose that this thing is a werewolf, or was.'

'A what?' I asked. At that time most of my knowledge was of a purely practical nature. Oh, I had read in my wife's volume of the *Complete Works of Shakespeare*, given to her as a wedding present. I had attended plays and recitals of music, and visited picture-galleries. The areas in which I had anything approaching to an adequate knowledge were all, however, attached in some way to the science of photography. I had not read sufficiently in the folklore of continental Europe to know what a werewolf is.

'A werewolf,' Sekt explained, 'is a man who

turns into a wolf at the time of the full moon.'

'But did you see a wolf?'

'Not exactly. But a werewolf is said by some people to look like a mixture of a man and a wolf, and to walk upright.'

'Was there a full moon when you saw it?'

'Actually, no.'

'It was daylight, wasn't it?'

'Of course.'

'Then it couldn't have been one of these things, could it?'

'Well.' He stroked an imaginary beard and shifted his position on the bed. 'It could be that the werewolf part of the old tales is right, but that the time of changing is just made up. Oh and, er…'

'What?'

'Well, I've just thought of another objection to the theory.'

'What's that?'

'The werewolf likes to eat raw flesh.'

'No interest in a nice cooked ham, then?'

'Not that I recall.' I wished Mr Sekt a good day, turned and made for the door.

'Even if it was a werewolf, I don't suppose it would stay still long enough for you to photograph it,' he said to my back.

'I'd have to catch it asleep. Or kill it.'

'Silver bullets,' he said.

'Sorry?'

'One uses silver bullets to kill a werewolf. It's the only way.'

I thanked him again for his help and promised to send him a free print of his most recent portrait. In the castle courtyard as I went out, I saw a group of students in their caps and gowns who were playing a hilarious little game. They had taken off their neckties and tied themselves together in a circle, by their wrists. They were obviously drunk, despite the early hour, and were singing some nautical song. They probably all lived in the castle, and couldn't decide whose room to go to. There were about ten of them, and they were all floating in a big ring from side to side of the courtyard.

This made me think of a new explanation for the presence of the 'werewolf'. A student, hearing that the Parisians were holding one of their artistic events, planned to ruin it by appearing out of the water in a bear-suit, or a monkey-suit. Unfortunately, his swim made him peckish, as swimming in freezing water often does. Instead of disrupting the theatricals, he stole the ham, not realising that little Sekt was watching him all the time.

I returned home to find that Mr Broadlock had left me a sealed note:

Minnie is much better after the efforts of your friend. I have invited him this afternoon at half past two o'clock, and would be grateful if you could come. We will meet in the foyer as before. Basildon Broadlock.

This time Harrison managed the short walk from his lodgings to the hotel under his own steam. There was no sign of his erstwhile supporters, Adah and Allan. He still had his wolf-headed cane, however. Although the American seemed physically better, he still appeared to be troubled in his mind. Broadlock asked him how he had managed to make Minnie so much better, but his answer was weary and reluctant. I cure the soul, he said, in essence. He must be weary, I thought, to turn up a chance to expound his theory to an interested person. Broadlock was of course interested intellectually, and of course he had a direct interest in his wife's health. Nevertheless, Harrison stared distractedly at his own pale hands and kept his lips tight shut. He cured the soul. That was all he could say, for now.

Basildon Broadlock, whose Christian name I had just recently learned, glanced at me, baffled. When he moved to go up to Minnie, I rose and instinctively offered to help Harrison out of his chair. He took my arm, and held on to it gratefully as we walked. 'You may ask what ails me,' he said, so quietly that Broadlock may not have heard.

'I thought it was colic?' He shook his head and smiled with a visible effort.

'Oh no,' he explained as we began to mount the stairs. 'Don't get me wrong, any conventional doctor would have concluded that I am suffering from colic, but colic is just a symptom. It is my soul. My soul is ailing. My soul wants to escape from this useless body.'

'I'm sure you have many good years still ahead of you,' said Basildon, as we reached the top of the stairs. He had stopped on the landing and we had caught up with him. He could now overhear our conversation. 'And in any case,' said Broadlock, 'death is just a passing over…'

'Who was talking about *death?*' asked Harrison.

'I heard you mention the soul,' Broadlock said defensively.

'The soul has nothing to do with death,' Harrison asserted breathlessly.

'The soul survives to escape the body at death,' said Broadlock, flushing red.

'I was not talking about death.'

Inside the hotel room, Mrs Broadlock was sitting bolt upright in bed, with a pretty shawl about her shoulders. I couldn't hear her breathing, though she did look very tired. The physical effort of breathing against the angry asthmatic knot in her chest had evidently been exhausting. Harrison smiled and bowed a deep, elaborate bow, with a touch of old-world gallantry about it. He touched the tip of his cane to his nose. Then, as before, he knelt down by her bedside. He then looked into her eyes, like a rather elderly suitor; or a doting older husband. She said nothing, but gazed back with an expression of complete confidence and submission. Again, Harrison generated silence as a mill will generate noise.

'Minnie, what are you afraid of?' Harrison asked, again. Broadlock, standing at my shoulder, stiffened slightly. He was conscious, no doubt, of having ended the last séance. He did not want to blunder into this one with an inopportune word.

'You know of my assistant, Allan Terris?' Harrison asked.

'I have heard of him,' said Minnie, in a cracked little voice.

'He was brave. He seemed to be afraid of nothing. He faced up to a tiger! Imagine that! But still, this brave man is still afraid of something.' Harrison was speaking in a low, deep voice, as he had before. He spoke very slowly, and his voice seemed to give out pockets of silence between each word.

'What is he afraid of?' Minnie asked, spellbound.

'He is afraid that he will remain himself to the end of his days.'

'How strange,' said Minnie, with reason enough for her words.

'I tried to get him to cast off his nickname, 'Tiger', but it hasn't worked. Even when he shaved off his whiskers, it was still him, waiting for himself in the mirror.' There was a pause, and the old Durham noises seemed to be surging up from the street again: the horses' hooves on the roads, conversation below the window, the squeal of block and tackle from the building site opposite.

'Speaking for myself, what I am afraid of is heat,' said Esau Harrison, looking down at the floor behind the bed. 'I am afraid that one day a stifling heat will come and burn me up like a faggot. Or melt me to death with perspiring.' This, I thought, explains his fondness for thin clothes.

'I sense that you do not want to tell me what you are afraid of. It may be you would tell me, if we were alone, but your friends have insisted that I should not be alone with you. But I have an idea. I want you to write your fear on this paper, and I will burn it with a match.' Here Harrison produced a small notepad and pencil from his pocket, together with a box of matches.

'Mr Blount,' he said, addressing me, 'you will be so kind as to empty that bowl of *pot pourri* and bring the empty bowl to me.' It was like an instruction from a magician to his assistant. I emptied the *pot pourri* onto the top of the sideboard and brought Harrison the china bowl. Minnie was already writing on a sheet of notepaper, in such a posture that nobody could see what she was writing.

'Now screw it up so that none can read it,' Harrison instructed. 'Put it in the bowl and I will burn it.' This happened just as he said, and the glow from the fire showed briefly through the china bowl. He had made no attempt to unravel the paper.

'She will be quite well tomorrow,' said Harrison as I accompanied him out into the street. 'She will be rowing her husband up and down the river!' I wasn't quite sure if Harrison was serious. After the séance, we had left the newly-weds alone and tramped back down the stairs, Esau and myself. My companion seemed a little energised by his healing feat, but still basically unwell. It seemed pretty obvious to me that some mental trouble was causing his outer malaise. 'Weren't you curious to know what she is afraid of?' I asked. 'You didn't get a look at the paper, did you?'

'No, no,' he replied.

'So what do you think it was?' By this time we were out in the street, and both of us bought copies of the *Durham County Advertiser* from a paper-boy. Harrison placed his, folded in four, in an outside pocket of his linen jacket. I tucked mine under my arm. As I looked up to see Harrison, I saw that Allan Terris had just appeared before him.

I had at first been unable to recognise my old friend when I first saw him without his beard. Now he was close to being unrecognisable again, but not because of any barbering. His whole appearance was changed because of rage, pure and simple. He was shaking all over, pointing at Harrison, and spluttering incomprehensibly. 'What's the matter?' I asked him. My friend ignored me.

'Where is it?' he shouted, coming closer to Harrison. By some protective instinct, I moved slightly to my left, so as to be ready to stand between them. I noticed that Harrison was no longer leaning on his stick, but had rested it on his shoulder like a rifle. I suppose he thought he could deploy it from there more easily, in his own defence.

'Tiger old chap, have you been drinking?' I asked. By this time the newspaper boy was gazing at us with interest. A builder on the scaffolding opposite was also watching. People on the street were giving us a wide berth and I thought I saw a young man running away in the direction of New Elvet, perhaps in search of a policeman.

'Where is it, you damned fraud?' Terris asked again.

'You have merely to wait until after dinner,' said Harrison, in his rich, compelling voice. It occurred to me that he may have been trying to hypnotise his assistant right there in the street, but his assistant was having none of it.

'You've paid them all off, Harrison. But there's still Newcastle, or Darlington, you know. Your nasty web doesn't stretch that far out, does it?'

At that time, I had absolutely no idea what he was talking about, or who 'they' were. Allan strode forward and made as if to grasp the lapels of the American's fine linen jacket. I stepped in and held my friend in a sort of half-embrace. By this time, a few more spectators had stopped to look, attracted by Allan's loud voice rebounding off the walls of the buildings in the Elvet.

Allan stepped back, not wanting to fight me.

'So he has *you* in his grasp now, has he, Jacob? You're his new disciple. Well, I'd watch out if I were you. This Yankee is nothing but trouble. He's the biggest fraud in the country!' With that, my old friend strode off over Elvet Bridge.

We saw him climb up the perspective, as it were, past the photography shop. He was muttering to himself and flinging his arms about like a madman. Passers-by who hadn't noticed the earlier altercation now glanced at Terris with looks of some concern. Harrison, for his part, looked badly shaken. I thought it would be impertinent to ask him for an explanation, although I hoped he would give one voluntarily. He did not. I saw him back to the street-door of his lodgings and hurried back home.

Chapter IX

The newspaper I had bought in the street contained some rather startling news. It seems that a retired miner, Billy Robson, had been fishing on the banks of the Wear early on Saturday morning. He had seen what he described as a 'git yep' ('large ape' in Durham dialect) emerging from the water. The creature surfaced in the middle of the river, swam to the edge and climbed out. It took no notice of Mr Robson; indeed it didn't seem to see him, but crept into the trees and vanished. I naturally connected the 'git yep' with the hairy creature Sekt had seen.

The new sighting had been at the very tip of the boat-shaped peninsular that forms the centre of Durham. It is heavily wooded and quite wild there. Anyone – or anything – could easily remain concealed among the trees and bushes, even in winter when there are no leaves. The ancient Prince Bishops of Durham had forbidden the planting of trees on the banks:

they didn't want marauding Scots to hide among them. In more recent years, escaped convicts from Durham Gaol had hidden there. When police attempts to 'comb' the banks had come too close, the convicts had simply escaped into the gardens of nearby houses, or into the houses themselves, or along the river to places like Finchale. One man had evaded police for two weeks in this peripatetic manner, but had at last been caught sheltering among the ruins of Finchale Abbey.

I had a strong feeling that there must be something in the newspaper report. If Robson had heard about this animal from a previous newspaper report, the *Durham County Advertiser* would surely have included some such phrase as; *'this is the second time the beast has been sighted - readers may remember our report of...'* I couldn't see how else Robson could have heard of the student, Sekt's, encounter on the riverbank.

Although the castle, where Sekt lived, stares down on Milburngate like a threatening giant, social points of contact between wealthy students and the city poor were and are very few. I was minded to think that the two sightings were independent of each other, that they corroborated with each other and were both reliable. I couldn't picture Billy Robson, a retired collier, sharing a drink and some talk with a pale young 'Aesthetic'.

If Billy Robson's testimony made it possible for me to take a photograph of this creature, then the picture might be sold to newspapers all over the world. A good percentage of money from the sales might stick to me. But how to take such a photograph in the first place? In those days we photographers still needed quite long exposures, even in bright sunlight. Wild animals are notoriously unwilling to stay still in the vicinity of a human standing behind a peculiar wooden box. I felt, though, that the beast might be shot with a rifle, or brought down with a blow from a police truncheon, and might then make a worthwhile photograph.

Meanwhile, the creature that Sekt had called a werewolf was a mystery – just like the contents of the note Minnie Broadlock had handed to Esau Harrison. I hoped that giving her fear away in that strange little ceremony would help Minnie to a full recovery.

As I entered once again the portals of *chez* Blount I was painfully aware that I had been neglecting the little photography business on Elvet Bridge, and that I would now have to buckle down. My semi-retired Uncle Eadweard had been taking on far too much of the portrait business, and had even been ordering in new supplies for the shop and the darkroom. He had also been developing and printing at night, when I was visiting my friend Mr Basildon Broadlock.

The shop was empty, and Hebe was taking a cup of tea behind the counter. 'Eadweard's gone,' she said. 'His Mrs Blount is having a big dinner party and wants him to get washed and brushed up properly.' I smiled. My uncle was always immaculate in his dress, but the rich city widow he had married got very nervous about such things when the time came for one of her special dinners.

'He says he's been working his fingers to the bone, and that he's only an *aul gadgie*,' said Hebe. 'Aul gadgie' is a local Durham phrase meaning 'an elderly person' of either sex. Hebe conveyed Eadweard's message with a smile, but I promised her that I would be able to work harder at the business now. Minnie Broadlock was, after all, very much better. The Broadlocks would soon be leaving for Newcastle, which had always been their destination. I would no longer be able to visit them so easily once they were up there.

About a half an hour after I had reached the shop, a young infantry captain came in and asked me to take a portrait photograph of him. He was about to go out to India, and wanted his sweetheart to have a copy of the picture as a keepsake. The man was rather thin, and I photographed him from below, including only his head and his shoulders, down to the third button on his tunic. I asked him to face our studio skylight so that there would be very little light and shade on his face, and a dark background. I made a mental note to print the picture inside an oval. These were all tricks to increase the captain's apparent weight as judged from the photograph. His sweetheart would be gazing at a picture that lied, just a little.

In those days, we used all sorts of methods to counteract unfortunate features of our subjects' appearance. Fat people would sometimes improve their appearance if helped with a little strong side lighting. Bald men would be encouraged to keep their hats on, or perhaps the studio hat stand (with a hat on it) could be pressed into service to cast a shadow where the hair had once been. People with really regrettable countenances would be posed against a very detailed background; perhaps a painting of the Cathedral with a lot of foliage below it.

I often argued with my uncle Eadweard about such techniques. He still believed in retouching with paint – an approach I had always disliked. We were both, however, trying to push our subjects toward some ideal of beauty or handsomeness that seemed pretty arbitrary in itself. The fashion in those days was for tight corsets and wasp waists for women (and in fact men). This had been the fashion for many years. When taking full-length portraits I encouraged women to stretch themselves and hold in their stomachs. Eadweard sometimes used to retouch the sides of the waist to make it appear narrower. Meanwhile, medical opinion agreed that this tight corseting was unhealthy, and, in a state of nature, few if any men or women could possess such narrow figures. Why couldn't the ideal of beauty be closer to the normal shape of men and women? At least then, those that were very fat or thin, or had some very marked peculiarity in appearance, could have a little more hope of attaining to normality.

I spent the hours before dinner stripped to my shirt, lugging heavy boxes downstairs. The boxes contained photographic plates, printing-paper and sundry other photographic accoutrements. After dinner, I organised the darkroom, ready for an all-night session of developing and printing. I deliberately made and drank an extremely strong pot of coffee, and got ready to labour into the night.

Since by now most of the tasks involved in these processes were quite automatic with me, I had time to speculate about my friend Tiger's altercation in the street with Esau Harrison. The only conclusion I could come to, based on his previous behaviour, was that Harrison had a secret supply of what we used to call 'ardent spirits' and that Tiger had been sampling them. Either that or Tiger had smuggled a bottle into his room at the Harrison flat, and that the old man had found it and poured it away. On reflection, neither of these explanations fitted everything that Tiger had said to the old man.

Harrison certainly seemed to have been in some distress in the previous few days, and I didn't believe that the physical cause was mere colic, as he had claimed. I thought about Adah Harrison's purchases in the butcher's shop. Perhaps, I thought, it was inevitable that Harrison's small ship of temperance and vegetarianism was bound to be rocked by the sea of a place like Durham, where much gluttony was to be seen among the wealthier citizens. At that time, I had no idea that the goings on in Harrison's flat comprised a sea-storm of Shakespearian dimensions.

Chapter X

At about three in the morning I began to become self-mesmerised by my work in the darkroom. I'd gone past the stage of tiredness, and felt that I could happily work on until dawn, and beyond, if only our cellar darkroom were sufficiently light-tight. The first sign of my mesmerised state appeared when I allowed a print of my infantry captain to become over-developed. I stood and watched it swimming in the developing-tray; my eyes dry as old onion skins. The paper became quite black before I realised that I had overdone it. I decided to give up for the night. I mechanically poured the used chemicals away and lit the oil lamp that stood on the bench. I extinguished the little red safelight and used an oil-lamp to light my way up the stairs. As I reached the ground floor, a sudden knock on the shop door nearly caused me to drop the lamp. My surprise was hardly less marked when I found a policeman outside.

He was in full police uniform, complete with

pointed hat, and with a bull's-eye lantern clipped to his belt. He also had the manly side-whiskers then considered desirable in an officer of the law.

'Inspector Maitland sends 'is compliments and you're to come and photograph a corpse,' said the constable. This sentence, with its large jump of sense in the middle, meant nothing to me at that time. 'What?' I asked.

'Inspector Maitland sends 'is compliments and you're to come and photograph a corpse,' the officer repeated, obviously keen not to stray from his text. This time a few little sparks of meaning flashed in my brain, but a large part of that organ was already asleep. Some of the remaining part of my grey matter was still working beneath my feet, down in the darkroom.

'There must be some mistake,' I protested. 'I'm not the usual police photographer!'

'Oh no. That's Jenks,' said the constable, 'but we can't get him to wake up.' In the greenish light of the gas streetlights I could just make out a smile on the constable's face. I took it to mean that they had found old Jenks dead drunk.

'Haven't you been to bed tonight, sir?' the policeman asked. I was not wearing night attire, but rather a long apron over my waistcoat.

'Working,' I explained. The policeman gave me the address in Old Elvet where I was needed, then vanished into the night.

I stepped into the ground-floor studio, where I quickly grabbed the big full-plate camera. I wouldn't normally have taken this huge teak-made brute out of the shop at all, but I didn't want to go downstairs again, and I happened to know that there was an unused plate in the thing. I took off my apron and threw on my jacket, which I had hung over a chair in the shop. I put the heavy tripod under one arm, and the camera under the other. At first, in my semi-comatose state, I seemed quite unconscious of the effort.

As I stumbled down into Old Elvet proper, I spotted the police ambulance outside Mrs Roberson's lodging-house. This was where Esau Harrison, Adah Harrison and my friend Tiger Terris lived. I felt very cold and very awake when I realised that one of them might now be the corpse I was to photograph.

I stopped to speak to Mrs Roberson when she put her head round her door. 'I have Adah in here,' she said. 'She's terribly shocked.' She was assuming that I already knew who dead. I noticed that another policeman was waiting outside Mrs Roberson's flat. Was the landlady a suspect? Was Adah? At least I now knew that both of *them* were alive.

I met my father-in-law, Detective Inspector Albert Maitland, sitting on the bottom stair. He was drinking a cup of tea. As I mounted the stairs with the constable who was carrying my tripod, his teacup was refreshed by Mrs Roberson's daughter, Alice. This girl, dressed in a long coat worn over her nightdress, had taken it upon herself to serve tea to the policemen who had appeared in her mother's house. The officers all smiled their silent appreciation. Alice herself looked grey in the face and deeply worried.

'Who's died?' I asked, stopping midway up the first flight of stairs and turning back to Maitland.

'We're not sure who it is yet, but it's not your friend Tiger Terris,' said the inspector, without turning round. 'That's pretty obvious,' he went on. 'We think Adah Harrison was in the house when it happened, but we can't get any sense out of her as yet. Possibly Alice's strong sweet tea will loosen her tongue.'

'Is it murder?'

'We think so. Everything seems to point to it.'

'Shall I take the picture now?' Maitland at last turned his head and inspected my weary figure, poised with a heavy camera on the stairs.

'Have you seen a dead body before, Jacob?'

he asked.

'No I haven't. Is it badly cut up?' I was thinking, of course, of the gruesome Whitechapel murders which had started only six years before. Some of the victims of the notorious 'Jack the Ripper' had been monstrously cut about.

'Is there a way you can take the picture without actually looking at the body?' Maitland asked. 'I don't want Hebe to accuse me of giving you nightmares.' So the body *was* cut up? I thought.

'You'd have to become a photographer yourself to bring that off,' I said to Maitland. 'In any case, I'd still have to develop the picture and print it. I'd still have to look at it then.' I rose to my full height (such as it was) as I said this, and stuck out my chest. I didn't want Maitland to think I was any less brave than he was.

'Have a shot of this,' said Maitland, proffering a silver-plated hip flask. I balanced the camera on a stair and the constable who was helping me rested the tripod against the wall. The contents of the hip-flask comprised a reasonably good neat whisky, grown rather pleasantly warm by its closeness to Maitland's hip. 'When you go in, see if you can't identify the fellow. We still haven't had a positive identification.'

I have a print of the photograph I took that evening before me as I write this. It is a large full-plate picture, with very good detail. I had not taken any flash equipment up to the death-room, for the simple and compelling reason that I owned none at the time. That night, I relied on a very long exposure, by the light of the gaslights in the room, which I turned full up. Once he had arrived, Albert Maitland stayed with me in the room, and watched my work with some interest. I know now that he was partly there to ensure that I did not disturb any evidence. It turned out that the exact positions of the objects in the room had a profound effect on the progress of the case. When all was ready, I took out my pocket watch, waited until the second hand reached twelve, and removed the brass lens-cap. I estimated that ten seconds would be adequate. After the seconds had elapsed, I replaced the cap. I do not remember taking the equipment home, but I do recall developing and printing the picture while a constable brewed up some tea in our little basement kitchen at home.

The resulting photograph shows a clean-shaven man sitting upright in an arm-chair, his eyes half-open. His face has a weary expression. The comparative crudeness of the chemicals of the time make his face look a little like a bag of white flour. He is wearing a checked suit of 'dittoes' (that is to say, the jacket, waistcoat and trousers must all have been cut from the same material). I had often seen Tiger Terris in a suit like this, but the dead man was much older and fairer than my friend.

As I have already stated, the suit was too small for the dead man. He had failed to fasten up any of the waistcoat buttons, and a thin line of white by the left shoulder shows that he must have split a seam while pulling on the jacket. There is a black stain oozing from beneath his jacket on the right side. This is blood – the orthochromatic plates of that period registered red as black. There is another black patch on his right knee. There is a small occasional table to the right of the man's chair. On the table is a carafe and glass of water, a scrap of paper and a pencil. As I handed the print to the waiting constable, I said, 'Tell the Inspector to put the end of his necktie over the bottom half of the face in the picture. I've just tried it with a bit of rag. The cloth acts as a substitute beard. The dead man is Esau Harrison. I'm sure of it.'

'Thank you sir,' said the constable, the side of his face lit by the dawn.

'By the way,' I added, 'do you know if there's anything written on that paper on the little table?' I had a feeling that he might tell me, although it was probably against the regulations for him to do so before someone higher up had issued an official statement. He was a little younger than me, and I had been answering a lot of *his* questions about photography while we had been waiting for plate, and then the print, to dry.

'If you keep it quiet sir,' said the constable, looking back at cellar door, ' it just says *I had to do it*'.

'And is it signed?'

'It's signed *Allan Terris*, but the Inspector noticed that *Allan* was written with one 'l' instead of two. Terris doesn't spell it that way, apparently. Anyway, goodnight sir. Or should I say, good morning! Thanks for all your help tonight. Just send your invoice round to the station when you have it ready.'

Looking back on my account of that morning's events, it seems to me incredible that I should have slept at all. I was after all full of strong coffee, and terribly overtired. I had just seen my first dead body and my best friend, Tiger Terris, seemed to be implicated in a murder. I did, nevertheless, sleep soundly until about ten in the morning.

I woke to a few seconds of blissful ignorance about Harrison's death: by this time my trick with the rag had convinced me that Harrison was definitely the victim. I stared at the familiar bedroom ceiling and fancied that it had all been a dream. The realisation that the murder had actually happened fell on me with the force of a collapsing house. I received confirmation when I sat up and discovered that I was still wearing my day-clothes. I staggered downstairs into the shop to inform Hebe that I was awake. I was about to go down into the cellar again when I saw Detective Sergeant Romilly entering through the shop door.

Romilly was about my age, and was Maitland's immediate inferior in the Durham detective force. He was exactly opposite to my father-in-law in appearance and character, being small, wiry and untrustworthy-looking. I had never liked the man.

'Good morning, Mr Blount,' he said. He looked me up and down in an insolent way. I felt very self-conscious about my lack of a collar and tie. I must have torn these off before retiring to bed, as a precaution against strangling myself in my sleep. I could also feel the hair standing up from the side of my head. 'Is there somewhere private we can go for a little chat?' he asked.

I took him down into the kitchen and started to make coffee for both of us. While I waited for the water to heat up, I gnawed on some rough oat biscuits. My uncle Eadweard was not about so there was nobody behind the partition, in the darkroom part of the cellar.

'I'd like to thank you for your help with our investigations,' he said, lowering his short, bony form into the kitchen chair (I was left with a stool). 'Since you are a friend of our main suspect, Mr Allan Terris, and since you knew the murdered man, I'm forced to question you about the two of them.' The kettle started to hiss and I was occupied with the coffee jug for a few minutes. As I waited for the grounds to settle in the jug, I asked, 'I'm not a suspect, am I?'

'Oh no,' he said. 'We just have to ask some routine questions. By the way, I should explain that Inspector Maitland would normally be interviewing you, but of course since you're a relative of his, that wouldn't be proper.'

'Of course.' I nervously poured the coffee into two mugs. Romilly took his with no sugar, but so much milk that it almost made me sick to look at it. 'Look here,' I said, 'I could get washed and shaved and you could come back… I mean…I just fell asleep as I was…' He sipped his coffee as though he disapproved of it in some way. 'That won't be necessary,' he said. 'It's just a few questions.'

'All right.' He looked at me with his milky grey eyes. His clothes all looked slightly too big for him. His expression seemed to me to suggest hunger. I would say that he had 'a lean and hungry look' to quote Shakespeare's description of Cassius in *Julius Caesar*. The strange thing is that this Detective Sergeant's name was in fact Cassius Romilly. Had his parents known at his birth that he would grow up looking like a hungry street-dog? It was hard to imagine him having parents, or ever having been a baby, at all.

'Mr Blount,' he began with a sigh. 'I have learned a little about you from Inspector Maitland, but I have to ask you these questions as if I knew absolutely nothing about you at all.'

'I understand.'

'Good. Well. You are friends with Allan Terris?'

'Yes.'

'Do you know where he is at the moment?' So he was missing.

'No idea, I'm afraid. He's not at Mrs Roberson's place? Have you tried his father's house?'

'Of course.'

'I see.' There was a pause.

'Mr Blount, I know that Mr Terris worked for the murdered man. Did it seem to you that they were getting on alright in recent days?' I hesitated, not wanting to condemn my friend. 'I'm afraid I witnessed an argument between them, in Old Elvet.' I went on to tell the police officer what I could remember of the altercation between Terris and Harrison outside the County Hotel. It seemed to me that honesty might be the best policy, especially since others had witnessed the confrontation. I could imagine Romilly hungrily tracking down every last witness and gorging himself on the scraps of their evidence. I didn't want to be the only one whose account didn't tally.

'How well did you know Mr Esau Harrison?' Romilly asked. I told him that I'd been to a rather disastrous lecture of his at the theatre, that I'd visited his flat, and had had a few conversations with him. I also mentioned his association with Minnie Broadlock.

'How would you describe his occupation?' This was a tough question.

'I suppose he was a sort of faith-healer.'

'Did he make money like this?'

'I think so. I think he was supposed to have cured some rich people, who gave him a lot of money out of gratitude.'

'We found quite a lot of cash in the flat,' Romilly told me. 'In American money and English money.'

'Really?' I asked. 'Where had he hidden it?'

'This information is all in the *Durham County Advertiser* today, I'm afraid,' Romilly sighed, 'along with a lot of other stuff on the case, true *and* false. I'm afraid Mrs Roberson and her maid learned a bit from the uniformed men, and then the women went and watered the city grapevine. It's grown all out of control now. The money was in two metal boxes, right up inside the fireplace. Somebody had gone in and knocked out six firebricks to make a hiding-place. You'd think the money would be ruined like that, by the heat, but Mrs Roberson told us that the murdered man never had a fire in there. Not until last night.'

'He lit a fire?'

'Yes. But not before he'd taken out the boxes. The money-boxes had been placed under Adah Harrison's bed. We knew they'd come from the fireplace because they were still covered with soot. They fitted in the hole when we tried them, and with room to spare.'

'Have you found a cause of death yet?' I asked

'Yes. There's been a post-mortem already. We couldn't use Dr Terris, of course, because his son may have been involved in the death of Harrison. It was Dr Codling. He says Harrison is by far the strangest corpse he's ever examined, but he thinks the cause of death was poisoning with Belladonna. There was a small bottle of it on the washstand in Harrison's bathroom. Anyway, you can read all this in the paper.'

'Sergeant, I'm still not sure if I am a suspect.'

'You are not,' Romilly said, standing up and putting his coffee-cup on the wooden draining board. He looked rather disappointed. 'If you were a suspect, I would have asked you to account for your movements last night. And I know you already know about the note Terris left by the corpse.' He nodded with scant courtesy and put on his brown bowler-hat. 'You do know that to help Terris to evade the police would be a serious crime?'

'Of course.'

'I'm saying this merely because I know that you are his friend. You know that if he so much as asks you for help, you must tell us?'

'Yes Sergeant.'

'Then I wish you good-day, Mr Blount.' With that he turned and rattled up the stairs.

Chapter XI

I felt that it was time to tell Hebe what had been happening. She had a right to know why I had come to bed so late, and why a police detective had just visited me at home. I came face to face with her in the shop, and noted sure signs of anxiety in her face. It turned out that she had been visited earlier in the morning by her father, Inspector Maitland. He had explained the whole thing. He had also suggested that she shouldn't try to wake me, since I'd had such a busy night. I couldn't decide whether she approved or disapproved of my nighttime activities – she generally made some sort of judgement on everything I did. I didn't have to wait long for her reaction.

'Oh you're in with the police now, are you?' she asked, turning her shapely back on me. This may have been some reference to thoughts of becoming a policeman that I had briefly entertained when I had first met her father. If a morose booby like that can become a detective,

I thought, then surely I can? I later realised that, though morose, Maitland was certainly not a booby. His character was more like that of Suworrow, the apparently stupid Russian general who had run rings around the French.

I decided to try to improve my appearance a little before we had any more visitors. When I had washed and shaved and changed my shirt, I went out for a newspaper. As there were no customers in the shop when I returned, I sat on one of the bentwood shop chairs and read out the details of the case to Hebe from the paper. She knitted her brows and crossed her arms. 'Your friend Tiger is not a killer,' she said. She said it with a sincere conviction that would have suited many a preacher I had heard. So convinced was she of her own intuition, that she did not need to back it up with any reasons. In fact, her conviction started to sweep away some of my new-fangled doubts about my friend. 'Is there anything they've missed out?' she asked, nodding towards the paper.

'I don't think so,' I said, scanning the front page again. 'But there is something new. They say that Adah Harrison has lost the power of speech. I didn't know that. It's probably temporary. It also says that a friend is looking after her at a secret location. I think she's probably just in Mrs Roberson's flat, as she was last night.' I looked down to the bottom of the page. 'And it says that the Inquest will be heard at the County Hotel in two days.'

Later that day, a note arrived from Mr Basildon Broadlock, asking me to accompany Minnie and himself back to Durham Station at three in the afternoon.

There was a very great contrast between our journey from Durham Railway Station with Minnie Broadlock, and our journey back to the station. This time, Minnie sat bolt upright in the carriage, smiling at her husband and myself. In her case, some trick of Esau Harrison's 'mentalism' had prevailed when doses of belladonna had proved quite ineffectual. Now, the remarkable man who could cure people in that way was dead. I suspected that the secret of his healing art had died with him – it seemed too spiritual to have been hidden among the slight pamphlets and printed lectures I knew he had published.

I remarked that the driver seemed to be taking us to the wrong side of the station – to the southbound rather than the northbound platform. Basildon Broadlock corrected me.

'We are going back to Croydon, Jacob,' he explained. 'I have sent a telegram to Minnie's friends in Newcastle to say that we cannot visit them now. I'm sure they will understand.' On the platform, Minnie tactfully drew away to allow Broadlock and myself to speak alone.

'She is really very much better,' I commented, admiring Minnie's confident stride. A few other men were glancing at her rosy face as well.

'Your friend Harrison has – I should say had – an extraordinary gift.'

'Indeed,' I said.

'Inspector Maitland, your father-in-law, came to see me at the hotel earlier today. He has no objection to my leaving. I have supplied him with our address in Croydon, in case he wishes to contact us again. I have not told Minnie about Harrison's death. I was interviewed by Maitland in private, and we both felt that the shock of hearing of a murder might cause a relapse in her condition. She wrote a letter of thanks to him, which I promised to deliver to him by hand. In fact, I just went out and walked around your noble city for a while. Here is the letter. Perhaps you will give it to his daughter?'

He handed me an envelope, then looked up at the trees in Wharton Park, the windy hill that lours over the railway station in Durham. 'Was he a religious man, this Esau Harrison?,' Broadlock asked. 'Where did his gift come from? Was it from God?' I felt that Broadlock had some concerns on this matter. By befriending Harrison, had he fallen in with some sort of demon? I wanted to reassure him.

'One time when I was in his flat, I noticed some books piled up on a table. A lot of them were religious books – the Book of Esdras, for instance, and Paradise Lost, and the Book of Esau. The Bible, of course.'

'That is a great comfort to me,' Broadlock replied, sighing. 'Those books show a broad-ranging interest in religious matters. Many people just have the Bible as a matter of form, of course, or as something to swear on, or out of superstition.' He glanced along the platform at Minnie. From the back, as she purchased some ribbons from a pedlar on the platform, her figure was now very pleasant to behold.

'It is possible, of course, that this Esau Harrison had a very close connexion with the Creator,' Broadlock went on. I nodded, but could not follow him at first. 'It may be that he was some sort of holy man, such as one comes across in India. Of course, we cannot even exclude the possibility that some kind of *prophet* might emerge in our drab modern times.' The train was now visible in the distance. Minnie was tripping along the platform to join us, folding her new ribbons into a tiny reticule. 'A prophet might go almost unnoticed in this mechanical age,' Broadlock added, the end of his thought surely suggested by the noise and smell of the approaching locomotive.

'A prophet is never recognised in his own country,' I quoted at my friend. Suddenly smiling, Broadlock declared, 'But this was not Harrison's country!' I nodded assent.

Regarding the train through his lorgnette, Broadlock said, 'Jacob, I will send a cheque for ten pounds to Mr Harrison's daughter. Money can be very tight when the head of the family has passed away.'

'There was quite a lot of money found in the flat,' I explained. He seemed to know that already. Maitland may have been picking Broadlock's legal brains during their private interview.

'My legal experience tells me that that money may be impounded by the police for some months,' said Broadlock. 'No, I wish to show my gratitude.'

Minnie had now rejoined us and was looking between our heads at the train. We were standing in the midst of a collection of good-quality matching luggage of all sizes.

'Mrs Broadlock,' I said to Minnie, bowing slightly, 'it has been a delight to be of service to you. I regard your husband as a very lucky man. I hope you will return to Durham soon. When you do, I hope you will let me take your picture. Meanwhile, I hope you will be happy, and blessed with many healthy babies, down in Croydon.'

Broadlock had stiffened in his posture. Minnie's face still had a ghost of a smile on it, but a kind of horror had entered her eyes, in response to my speech. My embarrassment was covered by the business of a uniformed man on the platform gesturing to the Broadlocks to get onto the train. Two porters put their luggage in after the couple had entrained.

Although Broadlock smiled and waved through the train window, Minnie sat down and presented her profile. Her face was, to the end, like that of a frightened child.

As I walked down the hill into the city I saw the end of their train vanishing over the viaduct. So now, I thought, I know what Minnie is afraid of. I know what she wrote on that paper, the paper she had handed to Harrison, and that Harrison had burned. I could see the whole story in my head: the young girl, young for her age, left alone in the big world. A big, older man comes and offers her her only chance to be safe. But she is afraid of him. He is so much bigger and stronger and older than she. She knows nothing of the world. She is brought back to his house in a big, noisy town that she has never seen. He sweeps her off on a honeymoon trip to another place she doesn't know. She has to share a sleeping compartment with him, perhaps. She cannot protest. She can say nothing. Her windpipe closes up in panic.

She nearly dies, but then she meets a man who looks at her, right into her eyes. Esau Harrison sees into her heart with his big, black eyes. She fancies that he knows everything about her. He isn't interested in her pretty face or figure. He looks into her soul and sees her fear looking back at him. Her fear is wrapped round her windpipe in the form of the serpentine Tempter of *Genesis*. To be destroyed, this demon has only to be named. As his name is burned, he falls into dust.

Chapter XII

The people at the County Hotel set up
Harrison's Inquest in a small ballroom at the
back of their ground floor: at ten in the
morning, the room was unlikely to be booked
for a dance. Some rather smart gilt chairs were
laid out in three blocks in front of the Coroner's
desk. The witnesses sat to the Coroner's left,
the jury sat to his right, and a number of
spectators sat in the middle. I think there must
have been about seventy people there, all told. I
had been summoned as a witness and I found
myself sitting across an aisle from Dr Terris. He
had a look of white-hot suppressed fury on his
face. He nodded acknowledgement to me, as if
frightened to speak. I felt sorry for him. He had
all but lost his son to this newcomer, Esau
Harrison. Now Harrison was dead, and it looked
as if Tiger had killed him. As if in admission of
his guilt, Tiger had now disappeared. Would Dr
Terris lose his son altogether, if he stowed away
on a ship and ended up in some Godforsaken

corner of South America? Or would the police find him? If so, wouldn't Dr Terris then lose his only child to the gallows?

The first witness was Mrs Roberson, who stood to one side of the Coroner's desk, the ends of her fingers resting lightly on a small table. She wore a good black gown and a broad new hat. She looked a fine figure of a woman, despite her years. She looked as if she might have been an actress, if marriage, childbearing and widowhood had not claimed her in her youth. It crossed my mind that her impressive outfit at the Inquest might have been her attempt to attract the attention of some eligible widower in the assembly.

'What was your relationship to the deceased, Mr Esau Harrison?' the Coroner asked her.

'He lodged in my house sir, with his daughter.'

'How long had they lodged there?'

'Oh, for a few months. Then Mr Terris came to live with them, just in the last few weeks. The flat has three bedrooms.' The Coroner paused and leaned forward. 'How did Mr Harrison strike you as a person?' he asked.

'Well, he was quite a character. An interesting man. An eccentric, I'd say.'

'I see. Did you ever have any disagreements with him or his daughter?'

'None at all. I didn't see much of him. Adah gave me the rent money and told me about his preferences in food, and so forth. The Harrisons were both vegetarians, you know, and Mr Terris was going that way.' There was a muttering in the ballroom. Vegetarianism was unusual, even suspect, as a habit of life in those days. It is hardly less so now, despite the example of Mr Shaw and others. The Coroner coughed to bring the assembly back to silence. 'When did you last see Mr Harrison alive?' he asked.

'I saw him come in on the afternoon before he died.'

'How did he seem at that time?'

'He was angry about something, I think. He stomped up them stairs very angry.'

'And when did you last see Mr Terris?'

'Just before that. He was going out. He looked angry too. I thought to myself, there's trouble brewing between those two.'

'Did you exchange any words with either of these men on the occasions when you saw them last?'

'No sir, I just saw them coming and going. We can see people come and go from the house through our bay windows on Old Elvet.'

'You said 'we'.'

'Yes, sir, my daughter Alice; she lives with me.'

'I see. So how did you come to discover that Mr Harrison was dead?'

'Well, that night, I was fast asleep, and Adah Harrison came banging on the door. Really thumping. And screaming. Of course, I opened up to her. She dragged me upstairs and there he was.' The Coroner paused and took a deep breath. He seemed to be trying to assess Mrs Roberson's character by looking at her outside. 'Mrs Roberson,' he began, ' had you seen Miss Harrison, or Mr Terris coming, or going to or from your premises between the time you last saw Mr Harrison alive, and the time you saw him dead?' Mrs Roberson seemed to run the rather long and tortuous question through her head to get it clear. In effect, the Coroner was asking her if she'd seen a murderer leaving the house. 'No sir,' she replied, slowly. 'But I was asleep some of that time.'

'Of course. And did you see anyone unfamiliar coming or going at any time that day?'

'No sir. I know all my tenants and their visitors. If I see anyone unfamiliar, I usually go down and talk to them. Find out a bit about them, you know. They might be thieves.' And you might be a nosy old gossip, Mrs Roberson, I thought then.

'Indeed. Thank you, Mrs Roberson. Oh, by the way, how is young Miss Harrison?'

'Well, she still can't talk. Dr Codling's been to see her. He said she should take a little bit of laudanum, but she won't take it. Then he suggested brandy and hot water, but she won't take that either. She just sits in the room (that's my room, in my little flat) and stares at the fireplace. For now, I'm sleeping in one of the empty rooms, upstairs. Alice is at home watching over her at the moment.'

'Thank you again, Mrs Roberson. You may sit down again now. Now...' at this point, the Coroner stood up. 'I have noticed that there are some ladies present among the company here. I am about to call Dr Codling, who has conducted a post mortem on the body of Mr Esau Harrison. He may have to describe things that would be upsetting to the ladies. If any ladies wish to withdraw at this point, would they please take the opportunity?' An old gentleman stood up politely, expecting the ladies to rise. None rose. 'Very well,' the Coroner said, sitting down. 'Then I call Dr James Codling.' The old gentleman sat down, muttering something about 'suffragettes'.

I hadn't seen this Dr Codling before. We had always relied on Dr Terris as our physician. Codling was evidently a newcomer on the scene, a very flabby young man with a ripe peachy roll of fat under his chin. I recalled a saying of my mother's, about doctors, as I looked at him. She always advised that one should choose a doctor by how healthy the doctor himself looked. A doctor's appearance of health is his best advertisement. It seemed to me that Codling had started life with some degree of good health – certainly with a healthy appetite – but had squandered this great gift on lazy living and overeating.

The young doctor coughed nervously and grew rather pink about the face. He arranged his papers on the little table and did a poor impersonation of a soldier standing to attention. The pose did not stay long. He was soon slouching again. He toyed nervously with his livid yellow necktie. From the expression of rage on Dr Terris's face, I judged that he thought Codling a disgrace to their profession. The Coroner started his questioning.

'Dr Codling, you conducted a post-mortem on the body of Mr Esau Harrison. Please give us a summary of your findings.'

Codling complied, in a hesitant, high-pitched voice that made one want to place no confidence at all in his testimony.

'I examined the deceased at four in the morning, at the morgue under the hospital. I was assisted by Dr Phillips, from the staff of the hospital. Mr Harrison was a large man whom I judged to be between fifty and sixty years of age. I noticed straight away that blood had penetrated through his jacket in one place, and through his trousers at the knee. I also noticed that his clothes were all too small for him.'

Codling paused and looked for a paper among those he had placed on the table. He found it, eventually, and continued, 'The jacket had the initials 'AT' embroidered on a label inside the neck. When we' took off the clothes, we noticed a number of small, straight cuts all over the body.'

At this everyone seemed to hold his or her breath. Multiple cuts on a murder victim still suggested the Whitechapel murderer to us in those days. News of the resumption of the Ripper's grisly work in London was then still half-expected. Indeed, I believe that in 1894 there were still sporadic attempts to bring the elusive Leather Apron to justice.

'How do you think these cuts were made?' the Coroner asked, impatiently.

'From their length and depth, and the straightness I have mentioned, it must have been a cutthroat razor. In fact we found such a razor in the pocket of the man's jacket.'

'In your opinion, were any of these cuts deep enough to have caused death, doctor?'

'No. There had been considerable bleeding from two of them, but nobody could die from such shallow cuts. The cuts must have been made shortly before death, though, because there was still blood on the cuts, and on the clothes, as I've described. Blood tends to dry and rub off a living person, eventually, even if they don't try to wash it off.'

'Did you notice anything else on the body?'

'Oh yes. We thought we should count the cuts, so we turned the body over. We were surprised by what we saw. There were cuts on his back, but also an extremely thick growth of hair between his neck and the middle of his back, spreading right over to his shoulders. It was impossible to see the skin through this hair – it was like a curtain. It was like fur, really. I had to search through it with my fingers to look for cuts, but I couldn't find any. There were cuts on the back, but these were all below this furry patch. I noticed that the cuts on his back were arranged, as it were, in a certain pattern.'

'What pattern?' asked the Coroner.

'Well, if you imagine the spinal column as the trunk of a fir tree, the cuts were arranged in a downward-sweeping pattern on either side, like the branches of a fir. By the way, we counted eighteen cuts altogether. They were all over the body, except on the head. There were none on the head.'

'If these cuts were not the cause of death, then what was, in your opinion?'

'I believe it was poisoning by belladonna.'

'Why?'

'A sure sign that belladonna is in the body is the dilation of the pupils of the eyes. This sign becomes fixed in death. When I saw the pupils in this condition, I examined the stomach for signs of the poison.'

'And?'

'I found a small quantity of belladonna in the stomach.'

'And how do you think it got there?'

'Well, in this case it seems to have been put into some drinking water. The remaining water in the carafe found near the body was tested. The glass was empty, by the way. But there was belladonna present in the carafe.'

'Thank you, doctor. Do you have anything to add?'

'No, sir.'

None of the ladies present had fainted or staggered out during Codling's evidence, which seemed to me to be more bizarre than revolting.

I should add that I recognised nobody present as being one of Harrison's band of followers in Durham. Perhaps these disciples, who were mostly ladies, had come out from under Harrison's spell as soon as he had died. One reads, in legends such as that of the Fisher

King , of populations that melt away into decline once their ruler has died or grown sick. Perhaps Harrison's followers, who expected him to heal them, grew disillusioned when he himself died. No doubt the more credulous of these followers would soon find a new refuge in revivalism, spiritualism, opium smoking, phrenology, rug-making, or some such craze.

Dr Codling sat down. I stole a glance at Dr Terris. His expression had changed. He seemed to be quite taken with this young Dr Codling. I was the next witness.

I'm afraid that the Coroner asked me questions designed partly to make me repeat facts already gained from Mrs Roberson and Dr Codling. Where I had to step on new ground was when I described Tiger's altercation with Harrison in the street, on the afternoon before his death. I made it perfectly clear to the Coroner that Tiger was my best friend, but he still listened seriously to my account. Perhaps my face struck him as honest-looking.

'So Mr Terris wanted something that Esau Harrison was hiding from him?' the Coroner asked. 'Something he couldn't get in Durham. Something he might even have killed for. Do you have any idea what it might have been?'

'None, sir.' Of course, I had my suspicions, but the Coroner had asked for facts.

My father-in-law, Detective Inspector Albert Maitland, was the last witness at the Inquest. He read his account of how and when he was called to the scene of the crime, from his notebook. He read out the contents of the note found by the body. He described the dead body as he had found it, and read out a list of all the objects that could be of conceivable interest to the Inquest that were found in the Harrison flat. These included the money-boxes from the chimney, the bottle of belladonna, the carafe of tainted water, the contents of the waste paper basket (nothing of interest) and the rakings of the fire (nothing but cold ashes).

After a lengthy adjournment, the Coroner read out his verdict:

'It is widely supposed in this city that the death of Mr Esau Harrison was brought about by the murderous actions of a certain young man. I do not feel able to make a statement on that young man's involvement at this time. There is no direct evidence linking anyone to this death. The man whom the police describe as their only suspect is missing at present. Please remember that this is a Coroner's Inquest, not a trial for murder. There is nobody on trial here – our chief concern is merely to establish the cause of death. I am therefore declaring the cause of death to be belladonna poisoning by person or persons unknown.'

Chapter XIII

The Inquest quickly dispersed, and I took care to get alongside Dr Terris as he went out. 'What did you think of Dr Codling, then?' I asked as we emerged into the street.

'He *looks* even more of a fool than my son,' he said.

'But do you think he gave a good account of himself?' Dr Terris thought for a while. 'In the unlikely event that I die under mysterious circumstances,' he said, 'I'd raise no objections to his examining me.' This was an ambiguous tribute, if ever I'd heard one.

'Really, so you think that his was a good analysis?' I asked.

'Aye,' said the little grey-haired doctor. 'These things aren't easy,' he went on; 'I've done it myself. In the wee small hours, assisted by some useless stranger, cutting up a big stinking corpse. I tell you, it's not easy. And poisonings! They can be tricky. A third of the tests you use will show positive for something quite innocuous, not just poison. A third of what you find is already in the body naturally, and the last third appears naturally as the body rots. It's a terrible job, futile much of the time. If Codling's got such a flair for it, he can do all the Durham post-mortems from now on if he likes. I wouldn't say he was perfect, mind, but he was a lot better than most.'

Dr Terris stopped himself rambling on and smiled a little. With the expression of a man making light conversation, he leaned forward and said, 'If you know where Allan is, pull your moustaches. If you don't, look across the road. You can trust me to keep it quiet. He's my son, and you're his friend. The police haven't even questioned me. But I want to know.' I looked across the road. His face fell.

I watched the doctor's back receding as he walked slowly home, and then I drifted across to where Albert Maitland was talking to three reporters from the local newspapers.

'We now have a cause of death,' he was saying, as they scribbled shorthand in their notebooks. 'We also have a sort of confession left at the scene of the crime. We have a reward out for information leading to Terris's arrest. When we have him, we'll find out for sure that he did it, and why he did it. He might also tell us why he dressed poor old Harrison up like that. Now we just need to catch him. And we shall.'

Maitland turned his back on the reporters and summoned Sergeant Romilly, who was talking to Dr Codling outside the front of the hotel. Together they made their way back to the police station, and I went home.

I believe that in the weeks that followed the Inquest, I became the most avid reader that the *Durham County Advertiser* had ever had in its history. I stepped out early to buy the morning edition from the newsagent in New Elvet, and scanned the columns for any news about Tiger Terris, or any further information concerning Esau Harrison or his daughter. I was so keen for news that on two occasions I wasted my pennies on the late edition, when I had already read the morning edition. In both cases, there was nothing new.

The only new information I discovered during my perusal of the Advertiser concerned the pharmacists around Durham. Apparently, several of them had come forward to say that Esau Harrison had spoken to them about his associate, Allan Terris. It seems that the American had come into all their shops, usually just before closing time. He had come with Adah Harrison. He had described Terris to the pharmacists, and warned them not to supply him with laudanum, or any other opiates, or poisons of any sort.

Most of the pharmacists claimed that they already knew Terris, who was quite a celebrity in the town at that period. Although only one of them admitted it, I believe all of these pharmacists were given, or at least offered, five pounds to compensate them for any loss of profits they might have suffered, through not supplying these items to Terris. I should have thought that five pounds would have more than compensated them – at that date, a skilled printer, for instance, would have been lucky to earn two pounds a week.

These disclosures seemed to me to throw new light on the dispute between Harrison and Tiger that I had witnessed outside the County Hotel. Tiger had said that he would go to Newcastle or Darlington to get what he wanted, to escape Harrison's 'web'. The web was perhaps Harrison's network of paid-off pharmacists, which evidently didn't stretch beyond Durham. Harrison had told Tiger to wait until 'after dinner'. Did Harrison have some kind of opiate concealed in the flat, which he was dealing out to Tiger at regular intervals? Had Harrison caused Tiger to become addicted to the filthy stuff, so as to have some kind of hold over him? Or had Tiger become a laudanum addict before Harrison's arrival in the city, and was Harrison weaning him off the drug?

As I read the papers, I also recalled the time I had seen Harrison throwing the Claypath pharmacist out of his own shop. Had this man reneged on his agreement with Harrison, and supplied laudanum to Allan Terris?

Despite the revelations about the pharmacists, the *Advertiser* soon grew tired of what they called the 'Elvet Murder Case'. Their crime reporter began to take a lively interest in new crimes, particularly a series of robberies from houses down by the river. The robber had never been seen, and he (or she) only stole food. The thief's *modus operandi* was to locate the kitchen of the house, then slip in through a door or window and take only food that could be eaten without further cooking or other preparation. Vegetables, most of which could be eaten raw if necessary, had also been stolen from gardens. A sharp knife had been taken from one kitchen from which a large game pie had also gone missing.

Chapter XIV

On a Friday evening during this period, I had an unexpected visit from my uncle, Eadweard Blount. He stood at our door in the darkness, holding a fishing rod. I was so surprised to see him kitted out in this way that I was temporarily dumb. He strode into the shop as if it were his home (as it once had been).

'What are your plans for tomorrow?' he asked, very quietly.

'I've got a couple of portraits, and some paperwork…'

'Never mind that,' he said. 'I'll do all that. You're going fishing. Where's Hebe?'

'She's in bed, I think. But I'm not a fisherman…'

'There's nothing to it.'

'But I don't even like to eat fish.'

'Nonsense. Nice bit of fish. Wonderful stuff. Anyway, this is course fishing.'

'What's that?' I asked. It sounded rather

rough, somehow.

'You throw the fish back, in course fishing.'

'But what's the point in that?'

'It's a sport. The sport of kings. I've got everything you need here in this box.' As well as the fishing-rod, he was carrying a wicker basket, very like a picnic-basket, with a handle and leather straps. He put the box on the floor of the shop and opened it. I had seen men fishing all the year round on the banks of the Wear at Durham, and I expected to see a sort of paraphernalia of hooks, flies, weights, lines and baits. Instead there was a large brown paper bag wrapped round what looked like a number of items.

'You won't be fishing in the city, or in the Wear at all,' said my uncle. 'You need to catch the train to Old Canch, and cut down through the fields to the river Brownie. Keep walking along the river for about ten minutes until you come to two dead trees. The one right in front of you is overgrown with moss and ivy and fungus. The one on the other side of the river is clean as a whistle and very white. Sit down and fish for an hour, and make sure nobody is watching you, and that nobody has followed you. Put this parcel behind the nearest of the dead trees. There are plenty of bushes to hide it behind. When you've done that, come home. And don't look back. I want you to do this every other day for the next week. Except that I want *you* to fill up the bag from now on.'

By now, I had worked out exactly why Eadweard suddenly wanted me to go fishing. Now I had only to explain to Hebe that I was going to waste several hours on a journey to Old Canch, to fish in cold weather for fish that I wouldn't even be bringing home.

The village of Old Canch figures largely in the history of my family in the county of Durham. It was in the Old Canch Mine that my grandfather had worked as a coal miner. He worked so hard, and so reliably, that he was promoted to pit deputy, a position equivalent to that of a foreman in a factory. He married late, to the village school-mistress, who was herself only in her late twenties when they wed. Only two of their four children, my father and my uncle, lived beyond their first year.

My grandfather was determined that neither of his sons would ever work in the 'pit' as the mines are known to the local people. The work underground was hard and dangerous, and offered few opportunities of advancement. When other men's sons went down into the mine, at the age of eleven, for instance, the two brothers Blount still had several years of school to work through. At the end of this prolonged education, my father and my uncle were both apprenticed to a printer in Durham City. My father stuck to the printing trade, but moved south to Croydon. My uncle turned his hobby of photography into a business, and stayed in Durham.

It is impossible to exaggerate the difference between life in the City of Durham and the coal towns and villages that lie just outside it. In the city, there is magnificent architecture, both domestic and ecclesiastical. In the pit villages, there are monotonous rows of terraced houses, unrelieved and unadorned. In the villages, then as now, there were few made-up roads or pavements; just dust in summer and mud or ice in winter. In the city, distinguished-looking people come and go, wearing fine new clothes. In the outlying villages, I have seen people of all ages in rags, or if not rags then extremely worn and dirty clothes. I have seen miners tramping to work in noisy boots in the middle of the night, their faces full of dread. I have seen the miners coming home at all hours, grinning through a mask of black pit dirt.

I have never been down a mine, but I know from talking to pitmen that conditions in those places are indeed very dangerous and unpleasant. Sometimes there is not enough air. Sometimes poisonous gas seeps into the shaft. Often it is very hot, and the miners wear nothing but a pair of shorts between their helmets and their boots. There is frequently damp and flooding, and sometimes the roof will cave in and kill large numbers of underground workers in an instant. I shudder to think that, were it not for my grandfather's determination and my father's good sense and hard work, I would have been born in Old Canch and sent down the 'pit' at eleven, with my metal 'bait' box (lunchbox) and Davy lamp.

My uncle's directions to my fishing-spot were excellent, and late on that Saturday afternoon I found myself fishing, for the first time in my life, in the valley below Old Canch. My uncle had told me that the fish would bite well at dusk. For this reason, I did not attach a hook to my line: I had no idea what I would do with a live fish if I caught one.

Above me, I could see the wooden fence that now blocked Old Canch off from the world.

There had been coal-mining in Old Canch since the beginnings of mining underground in tunnels, as opposed to the open cast type of mining. In the early days, the miners were not always supervised by mining engineers, and in Old Canch they often came too close to the surface, or ran two tunnels too close together. Over time, the wooden pit-props that were used to support the ceilings of the tunnels rotted. As a result, holes began to appear in Old Canch, around the time my grandmother died (she had been a widow for some years by then). At first people noticed depressions in the streets, and the square shapes of doors and windows becoming more like parallelograms. The bottles under the bar of the Collier's Tavern would chime all together for no apparent reason, as if a ghostly steamroller had just passed.

At last, a train derailed near the village. A nephew of the Mayor of Durham was killed in this incident, along with seven other people. It was put down to a rail having parted because the ground under it had fallen away. The Old Canch station and the rail itself were moved beyond the area that was now considered unsafe. This was a harbinger of doom for the village, but when a terrace of three houses collapsed, all at once, the authorities fenced the whole place off and moved the people out.

From the moment I stepped off the train at the Old Canch station, I felt I was being watched or followed. I couldn't see anyone suspicious, and I couldn't even so much as hear a footfall behind me, but as I walked down the bank to the river I was sure I was being spied on in some way. I had put on a very old woollen jacket, and my uncle had lent me a tweed hat with a fishing-fly stuck in it. These were sufficient, together with my fishing rod, to make me look like a fisherman in this part of the county. When a miner goes fishing, he cannot afford to put on some expensive tweed sports jacket. If he had such a thing, he would wear it to special evenings at the workingmen's club, or to the Methodist church picnic. A miner goes fishing in whatever clothes will keep out the elements, clothes that won't be ruined by a touch of mud.

When I had pretended to fish for about an hour, I crept behind the nearest dead tree with the large paper bag in my hand. I had examined the contents of the bag on the train – it contained a loaf of bread, a bottle of lemonade, some apples, a piece of cheese, some slices of ham, a newspaper and a pouch of pipe tobacco. On top was the bottle of beer that had been sloshing noisily throughout my journey. These provisions were obviously intended for my friend Tiger Terris. The elaborate, indirect and cryptic manner in which I was supposed to deliver them had been devised by my uncle to protect me. He seemed to think that I could not be guilty of helping a wanted man if he didn't spell out to me exactly why I was going to Old Canch. I could not imagine that this theoretical ignorance would wash at all in a court of law. One part of the mystery surrounding the fishing-trip was worthwhile, however. I still didn't know where Tiger was, although I suspected that he must be in one of the derelict buildings of Old Canch.

I looked about behind the dead tree to see exactly where I should put the bag. What I saw there shocked me so much that I dropped the bag. The beer-bottle rolled out and lodged under a bush. Behind the tree were the ripped-up remains of Tiger's last delivery of provisions, brought presumably by my uncle Eadweard. Some animal or animals, perhaps river rats, had hollowed out the bread, and eaten the cheese and ham right out of their packets. I could see apple-pips and the remains of the tobacco-pouch. They had even nibbled at the paper bag.

I assumed that animals would not have attacked the bag unless it had been left there for quite a long time. My uncle must have been delivering these provisions every two days, to guess by the amount. It was clear that something had prevented Tiger from collecting his last bag. I picked up the untouched beer and lemonade from the old bag and set off up the bank to Old Canch, with the new bag hidden under my jacket.

At the top of the bank was the disused Old Canch spur of the railway, behind a broken fence. All that remained of the railway was gravel – the sleepers and the rails themselves had been removed. As I stepped through a breach in the fence, I realised that it was nearly night. There was a long streak of red along the horizon in the direction of Durham.

There was little left of the houses in this first street, which was called, prosaically enough, Railway Street. All the windows and doors had been taken out, and all the slates had been pilfered from the roofs (we have very little tile in this part of the country). The street-lights had been wrenched out of the ground and even the gates ripped off the fronts of the little gardens. The village had not been pulled down because the demolition men had feared that their horses and engines would sink into the ground. Reduced to their skeletons of brick, it seemed to me that a few more Durham winters would level the houses without any human assistance.

I started along the street, peering in at doors to try and spot any signs of human habitation. The moonlight was now very bright, but it made very profound shadows. There was little visible colour, and I felt as if I were walking through one of my own photographs. Of course I became impatient with the business of peering into old houses, and started to walk too fast. When I got the feeling that I was walking down a street for the second time, I sat down by a hand-pump, which had been placed behind a long row of terraced houses.

I was thirsty, but I didn't want to drink the beer or lemonade intended for my poor fugitive friend. I tried the pump, and was very surprised to find that it still worked. It worked very well, in fact - the handle still went up and down with a smooth action. Somebody has been using this pump, I thought. Somebody has been using it recently. If it hadn't been used for a while, it would probably have rusted solid, or at least grown very stiff. I decided that Tiger Terris must have been using it. But why hadn't the water company turned off the water to this village? In theory, there was nobody here to drink it.

I remembered that the road sign for the street I was in said 'GREENWELL TERRACE'. Of course. This was the green well. Somebody had built a cover over it, and put on a hand-pump. A hundred years ago, or less, this had been an old-fashioned open well, no doubt with a bucket and rope. Now the march of progress had come to Old Canch, just in time for the village to collapse into oblivion. The water under this pump probably had nothing to do with the piped water that had once supplied the other houses.

I had read somewhere that the average man uses a surprising amount of water every day, not just to drink, but also to wash himself and his clothes (not that many men wash their clothes themselves). If, as I suspected, this was now the only working pump in Old Canch, then Tiger Terris could not be living far from it, if he was living here at all. It would be very irksome for him to carry his water over long distances one-handed, and every second spent in the open, for any reason, would expose Tiger to an increased risk of capture. I concluded that Tiger Terris had to be somewhere in the ruins of Greenwell Terrace.

I made a systematic search of Greenwell Terrace in moonlight, working from left to right as if the street were a line of written text. There was very little left of the first house, which had taken the brunt of wind and weather. It was now no more than a pile of bricks and rotten planks. The second house was better, but every morsel of wood had been stripped from it, so that it lacked a staircase and a ceiling to the ground floor. The third house was a little better, but the remains of the ground floor ceiling made me curse that I had not brought a lantern, or even a match with me: the ceiling blocked off what little light there was.

I opened the back door wide, and in the pitiful fragments of light that came in I saw that somebody had recently been living under the stairs, which remained intact here. This seemed to me a logical type of place to live if one had to live in Old Canch, since the staircase could act as a roof. As my pupils dilated in the darkness, I saw that the niche under the stairs contained a book, a zinc bucket with a handle, an unlit bull's-eye lantern and a pile of newspapers. I was so pleased with myself at finding this lair that I did not notice that someone or something had crept up behind me. In fact I did not notice this newcomer until he had given me a good thump on the head with half of an old floorboard. White spots seemed to jump out at me from the dark recesses of the room, and my eyes slid together, making me see double. I felt a cold stab of pain in the back of my neck, and I fell to my knees. I was still conscious, however. Perhaps it was just luck that made the floorboard so rotten that it snapped as it hit my head.

I pitched forward involuntarily and found myself sprawling on the floor of the ruined house. I rolled over, and lay gazing up at my assailant. The top half of his body seemed to vanish into darkness, and I could not identify him at all. 'I told you to keep away!' he screamed at me, and lunged forward with the jagged end of the broken floor-board pointed at my face. Letting go of the bottles and my other encumbrances, I rolled aside, stood up, and lunged at my attacker, who was screaming obscenities at me.

I tried to pin him to the ground. My proximity to him made me aware of his strong, unwashed smell. At this point I had no evidence that it was Tiger: for something to be visible in low light, it has to be relatively still. My opponent was squirming about like a rat under a boot. Nevertheless, I shouted, 'It's me! It's your friend Jacob!' and my man grew suddenly gentle.

He confirmed his identity by saying simply, 'Jacob?' Although his voice was gruff with disuse, it was still Tiger's voice, and the two of us embraced in the middle of the shattered floor. His shouting voice was so hysterical, it could have been anybody's. I smelt Tiger's unwashed odour floating into my nostrils again, along with the earthy damp of the old house.

'What are you doing here, old chap?' he asked. He seemed hardly able to believe in my presence.

'I was supposed to leave some things for you by the river,' I explained. 'I've dropped them down here somewhere. I saw the stuff you should have picked up earlier.'

'I couldn't get down there. But anyway, I thought your Uncle Eadweard was bringing this stuff.'

'He was, but he asked me to do it today.'

'Wait. Let me light my lamp,' he said, and I heard him rummaging in his pockets for a match.

Later, we sat together in Tiger's little niche under the stairs, sharing a pipe like Red Indians.

In the glow of his bullseye, Tiger was almost unrecognisable. His beard had returned as a stubbly black rash and his face had a look of latent hysteria that I found disturbing. Just a few nights of sleeping rough in this place had reduced him to a seeming tramper. I half-felt that I was sitting in Old Canch with a stranger.

I was determined not to eat any of his food, and I intended to give him the rest of my pouch of Virginia as a gift, above and beyond what was already in the pouch that my uncle had provided. I was also to give him my pipe – he had trodden on his and snapped it. I agreed to get his repaired when I returned to the city.

'Is this the first pipe you've had since you broke yours?' I asked

'I've been smoking tobacco rolled up in the end-papers of my book,' he explained.

'What is the book?'

'*Treasure Island.* I'm starting to feel like Ben Gunn.'

'Well, you'll soon look very like him,' I remarked. 'Black beards always seem to fill in quicker.' There was a pause. 'Why didn't you come to me first for help?' I asked. It was what I most wanted to know. He laughed in a dry, tobacco-parched way.

'You're married to the daughter of the Police Inspector in charge of the case,' he reminded me. 'I didn't want to compromise you.'

'Well, thank you,' I said with some reluctance.

'I think the trips out here were getting a bit much for old Eadweard. He had to ask for your help in the end, anyway.'

'I suppose one can have too much fishing, especially at this time of the year.'

'Did you catch anything?' Tiger asked.

'I did not. Why didn't you collect the last package?'

'I hurt my leg. I had to rest it up.'

'How did you do that? I mean, how did you hurt your leg?'

'I was attacked. Last night. No. A couple of nights ago. I'm starting to lose track of time. Do you have the right time there, Jacob?' By holding my pocket-watch up to the bullseye, I was able to read the time. I assured him that I corrected it every morning by the chimes of St Nicholas's in Durham, and he corrected his watch accordingly.

'Who attacked you?' I asked.

'There was no moon that night so I couldn't see him. Whoever he was, he was a strong brute. Hairy too. He picked me up and got ready to throw me at a wall. I reached down and thought I'd grabbed his hair, but it was his face.

I suppose I'll get a beard like that soon. Anyway, he still threw me and I landed awkwardly on my leg."

'Has he been back?'

'No. Perhaps he was just a tramper, passing through.'

'Are there other people living here?'

'I don't think so. Not permanently, anyway. I think courting couples might slip in from time to time. A couple of constables strolled round yesterday, but I managed to keep out of sight.'

'I see you have your own portrait on the wall of your residence,' I said, nodding towards the back of Tiger's den. He had pinned a newspaper article about himself to the wall with an old nail.

'That's why I'm not shaving. I'm clean-shaven in that newspaper picture. If I start to look like a proper tramp, nobody will want to look at me. Nobody wants to catch the eye of one of those sorry fellows. And you can't recognise somebody from a picture if you don't look at him.' His expression grew suddenly serious, and he searched my face. 'Tell me, Jacob. Does everyone in Durham think I killed Esau Harrison?'

'Pretty much everyone. But it's mainly because of your disappearance, I think.' At this, he looked suitably depressed. I handed him back the pipe.

'Tiger,' I said, straightening my back, 'I want to do everything I can to help your case. I want to make everyone realise you're not guilty.'

'Good,' he replied, 'and I'm pleased you don't seem to think I did it. But please don't ask me to give myself up. Many an innocent man's been hanged in Durham Gaol by accident. Even if they don't hang me, it's a living death in those places. I suppose they might even put me in a cell at Backram's,' he said, naming the local hospital for the criminally insane. 'That'd be a death sentence to me, as well.'

'Tiger,' I asked gently, 'did you see Harrison dead before you came away?'

'I certainly did. And a very strange sight it was. Some men would run to the ends of the earth to get away from such a sight.' I had to agree with him there. 'How's Adah, by the way?'

'Still in deep shock, I believe. She can't speak.'

'Trying to get her story straight first, I should think.'

'Do you think she'd have cause to lie?'

'Cause to lie? Jacob. Some people tell the most evil and destructive lies just by refusing to speak at all.'

''True. Do you think Adah is such a person?'

'Oh, certainly. And she's the centre of this whole thing. She's the axle and I'm the poor clod of earth, spinning round on the outside of the wheel. Her *desire* is at the centre of it. Her desire killed Harrison. That is, along with his mad notions. And her desire is going to kill me as well, if I'm not damned careful!'

'What on earth do you mean, old chap?' It crossed my mind that stress and isolation may have been driving him in the direction of Backram's, after all.

'What? Well...' He scratched his nose. 'She's the one who...look, I should tell this from the beginning, if I'm to tell it at all. Do you have to get home?'

'Not at all. We've got all night. Have a swig of this if it'll help.' I opened the bottle of beer and handed it to him. I was still determined not to have any myself. The contents of the Green Well outside would have to suffice for me.

'All right.' He settled himself into his place more comfortably. 'When I first met old Esau Harrison, it was shortly after he came to Durham, I think. I saw him in the Cathedral cloisters with that infernal Adah of his. We hadn't been introduced, but did that bother him? Oh no! He came straight up to me and stared into my eyes with those big fish eyes of his. "I can cure you," he says. Of course, I recognised an American accent. Behind him, Adah's smiling at me very nicely, under her red beret. I wish them both good afternoon and get away as quick as I can.

'Next time I see them, it's up in Wharton Park. I'm up there trying to get a bit of exercise, but of course I just get a lungful of cold wind instead. I see the two of them coming through the park gates, as I'm going out. He sees me and puts up his hand. He starts practically running toward me, and Adah jogs on beside him. I notice that, although it's very cold, and I've even got my old army greatcoat on, he's just wearing a flimsy linen suit. "Young man!" he shouts, "I know what troubles you! I can cure you."

'In a moment, the two of them are standing between me and the park gate. I want to escape, but they're obviously gentlefolk. Durham's a small town. If I'm rude to them now, I'll probably meet them in church on Sunday, or a tea party somewhere. I think this was how Harrison got most of his followers to join him. He just steamrollered them into submission. I decide to introduce myself, and he does the same. Then he draws me away, and Adah goes and sits on a bench under a tree and reads a book.

' "It is truly said, the eyes are the mirrors of

the soul," he says, "and I see torment reflected in yours." I suppose I should have realised then and there that he was some kind of quack, or spiritualist, or magnetiser. But you must realise that I really was in torment at that time, and suffering agonies because of my phantom hand.'

'Your what?' I asked. 'Oh yes. I remember. You managed to give me a good whack, even with a phantom hand,' I added, referring to our recent encounter.

'Yes. You and that hairy tramp as well.' He took a swig of beer and resumed.

'Harrison walked with me all over the park. He told me that the laudanum I was taking would kill me. He said laudanum was a poison. I was in awe at this point, because I hadn't even mentioned that my father had been prescribing laudanum for me. He said he could get me off the filthy stuff, and make the pain go away at the same time.

'That night at dinner I mentioned my encounter in the park to my father. I reported pretty much exactly what Harrison had said, and this made the old Governor go off like a grenade. Why was I idling round a park at my age? Why didn't I get an occupation? Did I have to fraternise with tourists? Well, you know what my father's like. He said Harrison was an evil quack, and had a damn nerve to call laudanum a poison, when he, the great Dr Terris... Well, I'm sure you can imagine the rest.

'Next day, I went to see Harrison at his lodgings – something we'd arranged in the park. I was determined to befriend the man, especially since my father had told me I shouldn't. Of course, some old patient of my dad's saw me coming out of there, and Dad said, "If you associate with him, there is no room for you here." So I moved in to *chez* Harrison, as you know. There was a spare room in the flat anyway. And by that time I'd already started to notice Adah.'

'Yes, I can see how she might act as an inducement,' I said, banging out the now extinct pipe.

'Yes,' Tiger agreed. 'I mean. She's not like a milkmaid type, with all rosy cheeks. And she's not a flirt, or any kind of coquette. You can't imagine her being a good mother, or managing a house. She's like something from one of Tennyson's Idylls. I usually go for blondes, myself...'

'My mother always calls Adah's type *pale and interesting*'.

'Well, perhaps a little too interesting for my blood. I learned a Chinese curse in India: may you live in interesting times.'

'So how did Harrison treat your illness?'

'He laid siege to it, that's what he did!'

'What do you mean?'

'I mean, it was just like a military campaign. First he got as much intelligence as he could. He went round all the pharmacists in the city and worked out exactly how much laudanum I'd been using. Of course, it was more than my father was prescribing.'

'But why take so much?'

'Because my father's prescription wasn't enough. Oh, it worked all right for a while, but then one dose wouldn't stretch quite as far as it used to; so I bought more. Then that new dose wouldn't last. You must understand – I needed the damned stuff to sleep. Soon I was getting all jittery just a couple of hours after a dose. And I mean a big dose, as well. I was drinking a lot, and smoking the old pipe and the cigars, but it didn't do any good. I was only really happy after I'd had a dose of the laudanum.'

'Why didn't you talk to me about this?' He smiled at me indulgently.

'Jacob. You're a fine upstanding young fellow. Just ask my father. He thinks you're a marvellous chap and he'd worship your picture if he had a portrait of you. I didn't think you'd understand all this. And I thought Hebe might get to know of it. I respect Hebe. I don't want her to know that I'm like one of those wretches who spend their lives in an opium den.'

'Tiger – you have more excuse than they do. You were in pain. Laudanum is an analgesic.'

'You just try telling that to my old governor. He said what he prescribed should have been more than enough. Anyway, it's not just an analgesic. What did DeQuincey call it? *Oh mighty Opium*. It's all the same stuff, you know. From the opium poppy. Poppies grow on broken ground, don't they? So the addiction grows on a broken man.'

'What did Harrison do to help you?'

'He went round all the pharmacists in the city again.'

'Why?'

'This time, it wasn't to find out how much I was taking. He tried to persuade them all that they should not give me any laudanum, opium, morphine, cocaine, cannabis; in fact anything like that.'

'And he gave them a five-pound note each?'

'Yes. That was in the papers, wasn't it? Quite an outlay. But there was a stick, as well as a carrot. He threw one of the pharmacists into the street and smashed up his shop. He had this stick with a wolf's head handle.'

'Yes, I've seen it.'

'The pharmacist told me about it later, when I went in for some cologne. You know, there's a lot of glass in a pharmacy, and Harrison looked like he was going to smash the whole lot with that cane. The pharmacist quickly relented and said he'd never sell me laudanum again.'

'Why didn't he press charges against Harrison?'

'He told me he couldn't, because he thought Harrison would just tell the police that he was selling some poisons without keeping a register. But I think he was just scared of Harrison. The man can be...I mean, could be, very frightening when he wanted to be.' I nodded, remembering the flying pharmacist I had seen in Claypath.

'I didn't know you wore cologne,' I said to Tiger.

'I don't now. I suppose I stink now.'

'What gave you the idea?'

'For what?'

'Wearing cologne.'

'That was Adah. She said she liked men to wear cologne, and she liked men to be clean-shaven.'

'So that's why you shaved off your whiskers?' It seemed odd to me that a woman, even one as eccentric as Adah Harrison, should prefer men to be effeminate in both their appearance and in their smell.

173

'Yes,' Tiger said, scratching his face. 'But Esau Harrison approved as well. He said I looked like a different man. He said his mission was to help me be born again, clean of all intoxicants.'

'So what else did *he* do to you, once Adah had put in her pennyworth?'

'He doled out the laudanum to me in regular doses. He also made sure I kept regular hours, and that he checked on me frequently in the day. That way I couldn't creep off to Newcastle or Darlington on a train to get more of the drug. And he checked my eyes.'

'Your eyes?'

'Yes. Laudanum makes the iris of your eye – the coloured part – it makes it squeeze up, so the pupil is tiny. It's called *pinpoint pupils*. The effect becomes more marked, straight after a dose.'

'I see.'

'He also talked to me a lot, all the time staring into my eyes. He'd tell me how bad I was in some ways, and how good I was in others. Sometimes he said my missing hand meant nothing. At other times he said I was a cripple, maimed, ugly.'

'Why did you submit to all this?'

'I was desperate. I knew that if I continued taking more and more laudanum, I would die. I wanted to break out into a normal kind of life. Not the army again. Not life as a laudanum addict. As a married man, perhaps. Like my old friend Jacob Blount.' I smiled and looked down at my feet. He resumed.

'The other thing was, well, Adah. I'd never met a woman like her. I grew more and more fascinated by her.' He scratched his leg. 'Living in the same flat with her was a proper torment, I can tell you. There's witchcraft in that woman, I'm sure. I think her eyes are just as mesmeric as her father's are. Or were.

'The only time we were alone together was when I accompanied her on walks to the Cathedral. Harrison approved of these walks because he said I needed fresh air. We would walk up Owengate, around the Cathedral Green, then straight through the Cathedral: you know, if there wasn't a big service going on. Then we would take a turn around the cloisters – that's where I had met her and her father the second time, of course. It was in those cloisters that she opened her heart to me. I remember it. It was one of those crisp, sunny spring days.'

'How do you mean, *opened her heart*?'

'She told me all about herself. Or at least, I thought then that she'd told me everything.'

'Allan,' I said. 'Can you tell me this? Should you?'

'I think I should,' he said. 'If you're going to be helping me, you should understand my circumstances. And Adah's past is all bound up in that.'

'Very well.'

He took a deep breath and stood up. He shuffled around the flatter parts of the floor in the moonlight as he spoke, limping slightly.

'She was born in a place called New Jersey, it seems. Her father was a poor farmer who already had ten children. Adah is very slim and delicate, of course: it was pretty obvious that she wasn't suited to farm work. They sent her off to go into service in the big city – in New York. She found work in the household of a wealthy widow.

'This old lady took an interest in theology and spiritualism and things like that. She was called something like Mrs Van Alten. Now, one day she fell in with our old friend Esau Harrison. He would come to her house and talk to Mrs Van Alten's friends about mesmerism, and miracles, and the power of the mind over the body, and the migration of the soul: all the stuff he went on about in Durham.

'Mrs Van Alten's friends were all old and ailing, Adah told me, so they were ready to hear about a cure, from anyone.

'The turning-point came when Harrison

cured Mrs Van Alten's gout. Of course, it may be that it was spring, and she was taking more exercise. Or maybe Harrison had persuaded her to drink less port and to eat less red meat. Whatever the reason, Mrs Van Alten thought that this was a miracle cure, and our friend Harrison became a constant visitor at her place. She lived on Park Avenue, apparently. That's a very respectable address in New York.

'When Mrs Van Alten had a dinner-party, Esau Harrison would entertain the guests by hypnotising the servants. He would make the maids believe they were back in their childhoods, playing in the streets or running in the fields. They would chatter away like children and spin invisible tops and so forth. He would also make the butler carry big weights on his outstretched arms.

'Now, you might think that Harrison or Mrs Van Alten had bribed the servants to go along with all these shenanigans. Well, Adah was living in the house with those servants, and she saw no evidence of any collusion at all.'

'Hold on a minute,' I said, suddenly realising something. 'Do you mean to say that Adah is not Esau Harrison's daughter? Did he adopt her?'

'Oh no. He first met her in New York.'

'So if he didn't adopt her, why does she have

his surname? Is it just a deception?'

'No. He married her.'

'What? She's his wife?'

'She *was*. Now I suppose, she's his widow.'

'I can't believe it. He's so much older than her.'

'Come come old chap. Lots of women marry older men.'

'I suppose so. But he wasn't exactly an oil painting, was he?'

'Indeed not.'

'But *why* did she marry him? Did he mesmerise her into it? One does hear of such things…'

'No.' He crouched down and rummaged in the darkness at my feet. 'When we've eaten, I'll tell you what happened,' he promised.

I protested that the food was intended for him alone, but he would not hear of it. I was very hungry by now, and my protests were very feeble. I promised to bring more the next day. He said that, after his fight with the hairy tramp, his leg was now sufficiently healed to allow him to walk down to the river and collect the parcel.

'I'm afraid my china and silverware are not of the very best,' he joked (he had none at all). 'But I must tell you that this beer is of the very finest vintage.' We ate hungrily and lit up another pipe to share.

'Apparently, Harrison could easily hypnotise all of Mrs Van Alten's servants, except Adah. He told the widow's guests that the girl had an iron will, and could not be hypnotised. He compared her will-power to that of Elizabeth I and Boadicea. Because of this, Mrs Van Alten and her servants began to look askance at her, and she found herself rather isolated, down in the servants' hall. But things got worse than that.

'That summer, Mrs Van Alten's nephew came to stay. He'd just been sent down from Harvard, which is one of their big universities over there. Apparently his behaviour had been so riotous that they didn't want him back. He had obviously decided to paint New York red as well as his disapproving *alma mater*. From what Adah told me, the rakehells of New York were more than ready for him.

'This fellow, Steven Palmody, sauntered into all the lowest gin-shops and opium-dens: all the disorderly houses, in fact. He arm-wrestled with sailors down on the docks, and he was chased by policemen all over the Battery. He cheated at cards in the homes of wealthy, dissolute bachelors. He jeered at all the latest music hall acts; but of course the Yankees call them vaudeville and burlesque acts.'

'This Palmody reminds me of a certain Allan Terris in his prime,' I suggested.

'I hardly know that Allan Terris any more,' said my friend. He continued his narrative.

'At home, Palmody's behaviour went unopposed. His aunt regarded him as a sort of visiting angel who could do no wrong – I need hardly say that she had no children of her own.

'He was a very-good-looking boy, apparently, with fair hair and angelic blue eyes. At last, his riotous times in New York came to an end. He was drinking with some English sailors and he happened to refer to Admiral Lord Nelson as a 'one-eyed limey whoremonger'. The English tars seemed to take this view of their great hero the wrong way. They used a method of physical persuasion on Palmody, to make him see the weakness of his opinion.

'They left him for dead somewhere near the East River. Some kind citizens brought him home on a shutter. In true New York style, they refused to hand him over until the old aunt had coughed up ten dollars. The doctor said he'd broken a rib and sustained a concussion. Everybody could see that Palmody was badly bruised all over.

'Now, she was frightened of what Harrison had said about Adah's *iron will*, but Dame Van

Alten had no more capable servant than Adah. Adah became his nurse, and lived in the most intimate relation to him for several months. All through the raging New York summer, in fact.'

'I think I can guess what happened next,' I said.

'Well, it happened,' Tiger continued. 'Although Harrison couldn't snake-charm her, young Palmody could. He found some personal chemical agent to rust her iron will. He was bored, probably; marooned in his sick-bed. Seducing her was an amusement for him.'

'I can just imagine what promises he made.'

'Yes. And no consequences for him in this world if he didn't keep his promises.

'But plenty of consequences for her. One consequence started to show itself all too soon.'

'Oh dear.'

'It's always happening to young maids. It's a music-hall joke. As soon as it became obvious, Mrs Van Alten gave Adah the sack. She wouldn't hear anything about her beloved nephew being the father. To her, he was just a young boy. In about an hour, Adah found herself on the streets.

'She was too ashamed to go home to the farm in New Jersey. She had enough money for a few nights at a cheap New York boarding house, but she knew that she had to find employment quickly, or starve. She tried the various agencies, but her condition was already too obvious. They couldn't recommend a girl in her delicate state as a housemaid.

'At last, she thought of Esau Harrison. He was the man who had complimented her on her iron will. He was also some kind of philanthropist, she thought. He cured people. Adah decided to go to him.

'She knew where he lived because she'd once had to take an urgent letter to his house from Mrs Van Alten. In those days, *chez* Harrison was some kind of boarding house for better-off people, rather like old Mrs Roberson's rooms here in Durham. The landlady there showed Adah up, and Harrison himself answered the door of his flat. Harrison observed all the proprieties, it seems, inviting his landlady in to act as a chaperone. When Harrison had learned as much as he needed to know, he arranged for her to move into an empty room in the same building. He took her out shopping and dressed her up in the sombre black outfit she always wears now.

'He also bought her a cheap wedding-ring. He started taking her out to the various séances where he was invited, or which had been organised for him. He passed her off as his daughter, which, as we know from his time in Durham, was all too easy for people to believe.

They were a very successful duo, accepted in the highest circles in New York. Adah's presence seemed to make Harrison even more acceptable to East Coast society. The constant presence of a daughter made him a family man, not just a solitary interloper.

'They explained Adah's pregnancy by saying that her husband had just died of dysentery in New Orleans. Meanwhile, Harrison went from strength to strength: he performed many apparent cures and was even interviewed by reporters from the New York newspapers.

'Eventually, of course, Mrs Van Alten and her set started spreading it around that Adah was not Harrison's daughter, and that the two of them were living in very irregular circumstances in a boarding house. A story that Harrison had deserted his wife began to circulate: the gossips said that he had left his wife to live with this younger woman. As autumn came, Adah and Esau Harrison decided to leave for Europe. They were married by the captain on board ship. Harrison had never been married before.'

'And the baby?' I asked. I had seen no baby or small child associated with the Harrison circle.

'Miscarriage – on board ship.'

Tiger Terris went on with his story for another twenty minutes or so, when I noticed that it was getting lighter in the shattered room. We came out from under the stairs and I got a good look at him in the full, unclouded moonlight. He was extremely dirty, as one might imagine, and the black beard-hair had grown almost up to his eyes. He was thin and tired-looking, with a lopsided smile of farewell on his face.

I should mention that, at the back of his little nest under the stairs, I had seen a metal box just like the ones I had photographed at Esau Harrison's lifeless feet.

Chapter XV

By the time I got back to the city, by foot, the morning was well underway. I slipped into my usual tobacconist on North Road and asked him to repair poor Tiger's pipe.

'I didn't know you had one of these, Mr Blount,' he said, examining the two broken pieces. 'Amber stem. Real amber, too. You didn't buy it here, did you?'

'Oh, no. It was a present.'

'Indian manufacture, by the looks of it,' he went on, remorselessly. 'Friend from India?' With a little feeble light coming in through his windows (which were quite orange with the tobacco-stain on the inside) the man's face looked oddly threatening. It was partly lit by the continual gas flame kept at the counter to ease customers' lighting of their cigars.

'Can you mend it?' I asked.

'Pick it up in two days sir. How did you break it, by the way?' How I hate inquisitive shopmen!

'Left it on the floor. Trod on it.'

'Oh dear. Well, it'll cost a shilling to repair.'

Just as I reached my door, I realised the
Hebe might have had no idea of why I had been
out for the whole night. I entered the shop,
which she had evidently opened, and she
flashed round the counter. She threw her arms
around me in a tight embrace, and I heard her
sobbing down in the middle of my chest. Then
she broke off, and, tears in her eyes, fetched me
a mighty slap on my left cheek.

I have mentioned before that Hebe was a
strong, healthy girl, and I must say that this
wifely blow sent me spinning over the floor like
an ice-skater. The pile of fishing equipment that
I was carrying thudded into the door of the
shop.

Hebe grasped me by the ears in a gesture
both tender and threatening. She spoke a speech
that she had probably been rehearsing in her
head all night.

'I don't know where you've been, Jacob, and
I don't want you to tell me. I can guess *who*
you've been with, but I don't want you to tell
me that either. I want you to remember that it is
a criminal offence to aid a man who is wanted
by the police. Try to think about what would
happen to me if you were put in Durham Gaol

for helping that man.'

She let go of my ears and told me that there was a cold dinner for me under a plate in the kitchen. She said that her father had come to see me in the evening, but that she'd lied to him (for the first time ever) and said I was working in the darkroom.

Despite all this drama, I climbed up to the bedroom and slept like a baby for ten hours. I dreamed a dream that rose entirely out of the last part of what Tiger had told me. I felt as if I had gone to sleep reading, and was going over the story in my head. The ethereal 'book' consisted of the narrative conveyed to me by Tiger.

In my dream, I was Tiger Terris, complete with missing hand and lately-lost whiskers. I was looking out of the window of my room in Harrison's apartments. It was night, and the gas was not on in my room. I could see the reflection of my face – of Tiger's face – superimposed on my view of the street outside. Somehow, this didn't seem strange to me. I was looking at people scuttling about under the street-lights at the junction of Old and New Elvets. It was exactly the view that Tiger would have had from his room at Mrs Roberson's. There was a fight between two roughs under a street-light outside of the Half Moon pub. One of the men was large and strong-looking, the other small and wiry. Yet I could see, as if with Tiger's own eyes, that the men were equally matched: the large man was slow and clumsy, and unarmed. The small man was nimble and inventive, and I saw his razor flashing in the gaslight.

In my dream, I heard the click of the door behind me, but did not turn round. The voice of Adah Harrison said, in a soft American accent, 'He's written his journal and gone to bed. He's asleep now. I can hear him snoring. I've finished my bath. Draw the curtain, Allan.'

I turned, and saw Adah with her wet hair clinging around her shoulders. She had a large white towel wrapped round under her arms. When I drew the curtain on the evening, she let the towel fall to the floor.

For the second day in far too short a time, I woke up very late and revived myself with a cold wash and shave, and the best breakfast I could make for myself. Before I could start to think over my dream, or my new information from Tiger, my father-in-law came to call.

'Are you fit?' he asked, when he found me clearing up in the darkroom. I didn't know what reply to give him. I had no way of knowing how much he knew about my recent activities.

'I had a late night. I trust you're well?'

'Oh yes. I just wondered if you were up to a spot of hunting.'

'Hunting?' I asked. I'd already been fishing.

'Yes. We've had another report of this ape-man creature down by the river.'

'Really?' I was relieved. The nine-day-wonder of the river seemed at that time to be a subject separate from the vicissitudes of Tiger Terris.

'A young serving-maid was taking a basket of food to an old lady who lives in a cottage by the river,' Maitland explained. 'The girl works for Lady Bagmore, a very charitable woman who lives in Hallgarth Street. The girl set out a bit late, and found herself walking through the dusk. Somebody – or something – pulled at her basket from behind. Now this girl is a Durham girl, and she decided to make a fight of it. She pulled back with all her might, until the handle came off the basket.'

'And while she was pulling, she saw this ape-man?'

'That's what she says. And she claims she hadn't even heard of the ape-man before. Not everyone reads the papers, I suppose. The description she gave was entirely consistent with the other reports – long, dark hair all over the face. She didn't see as much of him as old Billy Robson did, because the ape man's now taken to wearing trousers and a greatcoat.'

'So when was this?'

'Last night, when you'd locked yourself up in your blackroom.'

'Darkroom.'

'That's what I said.'

'So you want me to help you hunt this creature?'

'Not exactly. I just want twenty volunteers with long sticks to split into two groups and comb the whole riverbank. There'll be five on each side, from each group, and the two tens will meet up somewhere near where the thing was first spotted.' As he was speaking, he made a slow, vaguely fish-shaped gesture with both hands.

'But the thing can escape up roads and vennels,' I said, using the local word for the city's secret alleyways. 'It can get into gardens. It's been in gardens already.'

'Oh, we may not catch him, but if we comb the river-bank, we might find some clues, you know,' Maitland assured me.

'Like what?'

'Well, the remains of what it's been eating, for a start.'

'Why can't you get policemen to do this kind of work?'

'We haven't any left, Jacob. The Chief Constable's very annoyed that we haven't tracked down Tiger Terris yet, so he's got constables all over the county out looking for *him*. We're relying on volunteers for this other business. So if you want to help out, we're meeting behind the old boathouse at dawn tomorrow morning. And bring a stick!'

'Why dawn?'

'Well, we might catch him having a nice little doze somewhere. Don't worry, there'll be me and two constables along as well.'

Maitland seemed satisfied with my saying neither 'yes' nor 'no', and climbed up to the street. I sat on a stool in the kitchen and suddenly thought that this ape-man might be one and the same with the 'hairy tramp' who had attacked Tiger Terris. If he were now wearing clothes, it would be easy to mistake him for a tramp, always supposing that he really was some kind of hairy ape.

On the whole, I thought it would be for the best if I helped Inspector Maitland with his search. Helping him look for a wanted ape might perhaps make him a little less likely to think of me as somebody who might assist a wanted man. I would have to take more supplies to Tiger, this time by a different route, then sleep for a few hours with my clothes on, then join the men down by the boathouse. With any luck, Hebe wouldn't slap me again, especially if I told her what I was doing the next morning. Perhaps she would be pleased that I was helping her father.

I got up off the kitchen stool and looked on the scrubbed wooden draining-board. There was an envelope with the address written in Basildon Broadlock's handwriting. Hebe often put my post there. I slit the envelope open and read the contents:

My dear Jacob,

I am writing to thank you for your help and hospitality during our short visit to the beautiful city where you now reside.

I was distressed to read in The Times about the murder of our mutual friend Mr Esau Harrison. I hope that this business has not given you too much heartache in the period since we left Durham. I am pleased to say that Minnie managed the journey very well, and is now in good health.

In the spirit of my letters of an earlier date, wherein I was wont to try and educate you a little, I must tell you that your mention to me of the Book of Esau was certainly a mistake. Among the voluminous apocryphal literature of both Old and New Testaments, there is nothing called the Book of Esau. You might have seen the apocryphal books of Esdras in Harrison's study, or perhaps Ecclesiasticus. There is an apocryphal Letter to the Ephesians that was kept out of the New Testament, but I have been unable to find a Book of Esau.

Regards to Mrs Blount. I was sorry to have missed her altogether in Durham. If we come back, perhaps she and Minnie will become great friends.

Your friend,

Basildon Broadlock

I put the letter aside at that time, thinking only that it was very unlikely that Broadlock would ever return to Durham. He had practically got involved in the troubles surrounding a murder here, as well as having a very sick wife on his hands. It was possible that he might have brought Minnie back for another dose of Harrison's mysterious treatment, but the death of the hypnotist seemed to preclude this.

Chapter XVI

By the time I joined Maitland's Irregulars behind the Old Boathouse, I had carried out my plan of delivering supplies to Tiger. I had not seen Terris this time, as he had assured me that he would be able to get down to the river to get his supplies. I had also managed to get a few hours' sleep.

More men had assembled for the early-morning hunt than Maitland had asked to come. Perhaps the attack on a young girl (if such it really was) had roused some ancient spirit of chivalry in the men of Durham. In any case, there were boys young enough to be just out of short trousers, Dr Terris, and my spiritual advisor, the Reverend Dr Clement Considine. The vicar was wearing a tweed jacket, plus-fours and a deerstalker hat. Nevertheless, his discreet dog collar showed at his neck. The man of the cloth recognised me, and stared incredulously at my hatless head. It no doubt seemed like madness to him, to go out hatless on such a cold, foggy morning. I could not bear to put a hat on at this time because of the long, tender bump that Terris had given me.

I was very keen to have a word with Dr Terris, but to my great frustration, Considine got between us and began explaining to me why he was there.

'Break-in at the church,' he said, breathlessly. 'Terrible business. Communion wine gone, of course. And a Bible. One of my parishioners has told me that this Durham ape-man might have done it – my parishioner lives opposite the church and he saw something. Well, I've sent a note to the police station.

'So here we all are - I thought I'd come along and do my bit. I'm quite the countryman, you know, in my way. Long walks. Bit of riding in my youth…'

Despite his promise to me, Inspector Maitland was not present behind the boathouse, at this gathering of the troops, but his assistant Sergeant Romilly was there with the promised two police constables. Romilly gave us our instructions, and then sent half of the men across Elvet Bridge in twos and threes, so as not to attract attention. Eventually the rest of us headed downstream on the right bank, spread out in line abreast. The other half of our search party would cut across the base of the peninsular and get down to the river on the other side. They would work their way round until we met up with them.

To get round any insurmountable land obstacles, four of the largest boats that were commonly rented out from the boathouse followed us, two to each party. We would be rowed past any places we could not traverse on foot. When a handful of men had crossed the bridge to search the left bank on our side of the peninsular, we were ready.

I found myself between the Reverend Dr Considine and one of the constables. Dr Terris was three or four men away from me. We all shuffled forward at a deliberate pace, poking in the grass and weeds underfoot with our sticks for any clues. I found some beer-bottles, cigarette- and cigar- stubs and handbills for a performance at the theatre. These things could have belonged to anyone. In our eagerness, we began to speed up as we passed through the misty morning. The constable told us to slow down. 'It isn't a race,' he said.

Despite the fact that we were now proceeding very slowly again, Dr Considine quickly got out of breath. He twisted his ankle slightly as well. We were, after all, walking along the side of a steep, wooded bank. The ground was very uneven. Considine made it known that he had had enough, and I was obliged to help him to the famous Count's

House, where we both sat down. Around us, the mist was beginning to clear. Most of what remained was clinging to the glassy surface of the river. Considine took off his boot and manipulated his ankle. It was clear that I would have to wait with him, and support his arm on the way home.

'I'm terribly sorry,' he said. 'I thought I'd be up to this. I suppose I have to face the fact that I'm not a young man any more. You go on. Catch up with the rest,' he suggested half-heartedly. I said I was tired too, and that I didn't think they'd find anything anyway. I looked inside the Count's House, which is a little ornamental Greek temple, as I have already said. There were signs that somebody had lit a small fire in there, but not recently. The ashes were cold and damp.

'How are you getting on with your reading?' asked Considine. He was referring to the books he had lent me as part of my preparation for Confirmation in the Anglican Church.

'I'm finding it most interesting,' I lied. Having now fulfilled his obligation to enquire about my studies, Considine changed the subject.

'What do you think this ape-man is?' he asked, looking about him with ill-concealed apprehension.

'I think it's just a tramp with a big beard. And a low forehead, you know.'

'It's possible. But two people have had a clear look at him. The maid got quite a prolonged look at him in pretty good light. One is always seeing men who are too poor or too idle to shave or trim their beards. But they don't look like apes.'

'What if it's a lunatic escaped from Winterton Hospital?' I asked.

'Well yes, I suppose so. There are such things as microcephalic idiots. They are born with brains much smaller than the average. They might have a correspondingly small skull...' Considine was showing that he had read widely outside of theology, the Bible and parish circulars.

'Perhaps that would make them look like apes, because I suppose they wouldn't have large foreheads,' I speculated. Considine nodded.

'They may in fact be so wild that the staff at Winterton wouldn't be able to get near enough to do any shaving or hair-cutting,' he said, with a slight shiver of his shoulders.

'But there have been no reports of any escapes from Winterton.'

'Perhaps their escaped patient is of such a strange type that they're afraid to admit that he *has* escaped. They might even be afraid to admit that that type of patient ever existed.'

'How do you mean?' I asked.

'I mean that in the current climate of speculation about...well, about the descent of man, the existence of...such a patient...might be extremely inflammatory.'

'What?' Considine had lost me. He took a deep breath.

'There are wild-men, hairy men, the Green Man, in the mythology and literature of many races, over thousands of years.'

'Yes?'

'Whenever they discover a new species of ape somewhere, they find that the local human beings regard them as people like themselves.'

'Really? I didn't know that.'

'Oh yes. It's often the case. And of course there are cases of children abandoned in the forest, who have been brought up by wild animals – such as wolves.'

'Yes. I've heard of such cases.'

'Just think about our own English literature. Ben Jonson wrote a little play about hairy men visiting from the Moon. Shakespeare wrote about Caliban. Swift wrote about the savage yahoos. And what of Mr Stephenson's revolting Hyde? In the Bible we have Esau, the hairy son of Isaac in Genesis…' Considine seemed to me to be beating about at least one bush.

'So what do you conclude from all this?' I asked, trying to drag him from his well-beaten metaphorical bushes.

'Well, I mean that if Mr Darwin is right,' he said, leaning forward, 'some hairy ape ancestor might still be living among us.' It was an exciting idea, but I had my doubts.

'He can't be that far from human,' I argued. 'He took a Bible, didn't he? That is, assuming that your parishioner saw him aright.' Considine shook his head.

'If he's from Winterton, he might have got hold of some notion that the Bible is magic – a superstitious idea that it will give him magic and power.'

'True. And the communion wine?'

'I've seen men turned into beasts by drink in this city. Perhaps my thief is a beast who will make himself more beastly through drink.'

'Are you sure your theft was perpetrated by this ape-man?' I asked.

'St Matthew's is very easily accessible from the river. In fact, some of my parishioners get to church that way on a Sunday morning, in dry weather. All of the ape-man's thefts have happened near the river,' he reminded me. We both fell to thinking, as the old cleric recouped his strength.

I thought it prudent not to tell Considine about the attack on Tiger Terris, far from the Wear at Old Canch. I smiled at this unlikely reader of Darwin, and stood up. I could still feel the shape of the stone ledge I had been sitting on, on my fundamental part. I walked along the wall behind the Count's house, scraping the stones with my stick.

It was a wall like many others in the city, made from the very soft, warm-coloured Durham Levels stone, in this case worn as soft as unvarnished *papier mache*. There was one part that seemed more broken-down than the rest. The ivy that had grown all over the rest of the wall was not present in this patch. Likewise, there was a slight depression in the top edge of the wall. It looked as if someone had recently been climbing over the wall, and very frequently at that.

I turned back to Considine, and found that he had started off down to the river. 'I'm going home,' he cried, when he saw me. The flatter ground near the Wear would be better for his delicate ankle.

I am aware that I should have alerted Sergeant Romilly and his party to the fact that I was climbing into a private garden, but they were a long way away by this time. I was filled with a childish curiosity as well. I tried to insert the toe of my boot into the ragged gap between two stones, and watched my foot disappear into a generous hole. On closer inspection, I found that this was a foothold, deliberately cut into the stone, probably with another stone or a brick.

Perhaps, I thought, this is a convenient climbing-place for boys in search of apples to steal. It has long been a commonplace among boys in England that all apples, whether grown in gardens or orchards, will go to waste unless taken without the growers' permission by venturesome 'scrumpers'. But the marks on the wall were recent, and the apples this far north, and at this time of year, would be quite non-existent.

Boosting myself with a push of the foot I had lodged in the wall, I hooked my hands over the top. I was immediately aware of a silent avalanche of stone-dust, moss, lichen and dirt that would all have to be brushed off my clothes before Hebe saw them. I swung my leg over and sat astride the top of the wall, looking down on a scene of vegetation in the last degree of chaotic neglect. Some lines from Tennyson came into my head as I looked down:

With blackest moss the flower-pots
Were thickly crusted, one and all:
The rusted nails fell from the knots

That held the pear to the gable-wall...

At one time, this had been a well-organised garden, with a lawn, exotic bushes and carefully pruned trees. Now the stronger plants had subdued the more delicate ones, and the trees had grown out into great dark umbrellas. Not one of the trees was an apple tree, as it happened. The garden was unnaturally dark. In the midst, the basin of a stone fountain had been rendered nearly invisible by overgrown grass. At the top of the fountain, the figure of a woman carrying a ewer had developed thick mossy epaulettes. I noticed another statue locked in the embrace of a giant briar.

The second statue was a representation of the famous little Polish Count of Durham, complete with his miniature tailcoat and watch-chain. I guessed that this figure was actual size. It stood on a plinth that I think put his eyes somewhere near the average height for a man (it was hard to tell for sure – I couldn't see the ground).

I recalled that the house in front of this garden was owned by an eccentric beneficiary of the Little Count's will. Mochnacki, a Polish nephew of the Count, lived in this large house, without servants. His food and some other supplies were brought to the house by delivery boys. For years nobody had seen the man, except for the butcher's boy, the grocer's boy, etc. All the windows of the house were kept permanently shuttered.

As it happened, I had taken Mochnacki's picture only six weeks or so before I found myself standing in his garden. He had required me to come to his house with my camera and tripod. I had flung open some shutters that were practically glued together by cobwebs. The light streamed in on a short, white-haired man in a smart black suit. By 'short' I mean that he was well under five feet; he was nothing like as tiny as his famous uncle, who measured only three feet and three inches in height.

Mochnacki was very affable with me, and apologised for the dust that lay like a grey snow on every surface. He explained that the picture was to be sent to his sweetheart in Poland. She would send a picture in reply. This all seemed very quaint from a man who looked to be well over sixty years of age. I had no hint of the age of the sweetheart. Whether the Pole disliked her picture, or she his, I never found out. In any case, I never heard that a Mrs Mochnacki had been installed at the shuttered house.

As I sat on the wall, my attention was drawn to the remains of a glasshouse near to one wall of the garden. Most of its glass seemed to be missing, and the remaining glass was smeared with a growth of greenish slime.

I dropped down from the wall onto a floor of

overgrown grass, knot-weed and dead leaves. I glanced up at the house. In theory, I should have gone round and knocked on the door of the place, to ask permission to explore the garden. I thought, however, that my knock would not be answered, and that, in any case, nobody would ever be able to see me through the window-shutters.

The remaining glass in the glasshouse formed a sort of open tent at one end of it. Instead of rows of miniature plant-pots on wooden benches, I found two blankets, neatly folded, and a sort of canvas oilcloth. There were some empty wine-bottles and, hung from a string, Mr Considine's Bible. Outside the sheltered part of this lodging a tidy little hearth had been made from a few flat stones. The arrangement of these effects spoke of a degree of civilisation and intelligence in the arranger. Would an ape or an idiot hang up a Bible to save it from damp?

Between the glasshouse and the blind house itself there was a sort of ragged hedge formed from half a dozen rampant bushes. I calculated that, once over the wall, the occupant of the glasshouse would never be seen by his neighbour in the house proper, unless the eccentric Pole was in the habit of walking in his own garden. From the wild state of the garden, I guessed that Mochnacki never walked there.

The glasshouse was, moreover, a long way from the house. If the ape-man lit his fire at night, and had a care for the direction of the wind, someone inside the house need never smell the fire. The rest of the street would, of course, be giving out the sulphurous smell of their own big coal fires, masking the smell of the ape-man's camp-fire.

This whole hideout was completely invisible from the other side of the garden wall. Inside the garden, I had the strange feeling that I was in another world.

I decided not to risk discovery by walking round the house onto the street. Instead, I climbed back over the wall and walked along the river, hoping to come across Sergeant Romilly. As I approached him and his band of searchers, it occurred to me that, by telling everyone at once, I might occasion a mass invasion of Mr Mochnacki's property. This might upset Mr Mochnacki. It would also wreck any evidence that could be gleaned from the objects the ape-man had left in his strange glass tepee. Instead, I sat with the searchers and looked over the objects they had found.

There were several bottles, none of them bearing labels such as would indicate that they had once contained communion wine. The most relevant artefact that the searchers had upturned was a large leg-bone from a pig – probably the remains of the ham stolen by the ape-man. As Romilly pointed out, in his dry way, it proved absolutely nothing except that at some time in the recent past somebody had dumped the bone near the river. Nobody could say whose pig-bone it had once been.

After much smoking and shaking of heads the searchers broke up, probably relieved not to have encountered the ape-man, already an object of fear in the town. I waylaid Romilly when I could get him on his own, and told him about my find.

'You didn't touch anything?' he asked, frowning.

'No.'

'You didn't speak to the Polack?'

'No. I didn't even see him. Do you want to take a look?'

'Not at the moment. I'm not interested in clues. I want to *catch* the hairy little devil. If your footprints in the grass aren't too obvious, the ape-man might not realise anyone's been there.'

'So you will lie in wait for him?'

'Exactly. Now of course, you know you were breaking the law when you went into that garden?'

'Yes, I suppose I was.'

'So really, you shouldn't tell anyone about your little adventure. And the police can't go in there without the owner's permission, or a warrant.'

'You know that the owner's a recluse?'

'Yes,' said Romilly, 'I've heard about that. Still, it shouldn't take long to get a warrant.'

He strode off, neglecting to thank me for my crucial new information.

Chapter XVII

At home, Hebe greeted me with a nod as I came in through the shop. She looked worried. Her father, Inspector Albert Maitland, was waiting for me upstairs, drinking tea in our little dining room. As soon as I entered, he shut all the doors and pushed me down into one of the dining-room chairs.

'I had my doubts about my daughter marrying a foreigner,' he said, towering over me. 'I didn't realise she was marrying a bloody fool.' (Foreigner is a word sometimes used by the hospitable people of the north-east to describe their countrymen who happen to come from outside of their region. The problem with the use of this word is that it leaves no words over to describe people from other countries.)

'What are you talking about?' I asked, although of course I had my suspicions.

'I'm talking about this.' To my immense dismay, he produced Tiger Terris's amber-stemmed pipe from his pocket. The thing had been very skilfully repaired, so that I could hardly see the join. As it happened, I had returned this pipe to Tiger in his paper bag of supplies during the previous night.

'So you have Allan?' I asked

'Of course,' Maitland said with a trace of regret. 'The tobacconist who repaired it is a law-abiding subject of Her Majesty Queen Victoria. He told me you'd brought the broken pipe in, but he knew it wasn't yours. He could tell it had been made in India, and he knew Tiger Terris had been to that country. He also knew that you two were friends.'

'So you had me followed?'

'Of course.'

'I suppose you have to arrest me now?' Maitland pinched his right ear lobe.

'I mentioned that the tobacconist is a loyal subject of the Queen. He's also a man who can keep a secret. In a small city like this, that is an important skill. I've asked him to keep quiet about all this. And I bought five big cigars while I was asking him to keep quiet. Cost me a fortune. But I'm pretty sure he won't talk now.'

'So you're protecting me?' I asked. I stood up, dodging out of Maitland's shadow, and made for the whisky decanter.

'Yes,' Maitland replied, watching me carefully as I set out two glasses. 'Though you don't deserve it,' he added. 'We'll say there was an anonymous witness to Tiger's presence in Old Canch. Someone who won't come forward as a witness in court, and who just mentioned Tiger's whereabouts to me as I was strolling about the city.'

It occurred to me that Maitland would thus be credited with finding Terris, and that Sergeant Romilly was now going to get the credit for the discovery of the ape-man's lair. In truth, I was responsible, in a way, for both discoveries, but my presence at both hideouts had made me a criminal. I thought of my abortive career as a burglar in Croydon and determined to keep out of any more such entanglements in future. Maitland took the very generous helping of Scotch that I handed to him.

'I'm protecting you because I've lost a wife, and I don't want to lose a daughter as well. Hebe's as stubborn as her mother, and if I lock you away, she'll never speak to me again. And I know your uncle's also involved. If I arrest you, he'll get dragged down as well.'

'What if Tiger is innocent?' I asked.

'What?'

'What if Tiger is innocent?'

'How can he be innocent? He ran away and hid in that Godforsaken place for days. Now listen.'

'Yes.'

'I want you to keep as far away from this case as you can. If you're called as a witness in the trial, then just do your best. But you mustn't visit Tiger in prison, or send him anything, or even talk about the case to anyone. If somebody brings it up, just change the subject, quick as you can. Do you understand?'

'Yes, father-in-law.' We clinked our glasses together, although he had already nearly finished his.

'Remember,' he added, 'it was an anonymous tip-off.'

We sat together at the dining-room table and put our glasses on the green velvet table-cover. He told me about Tiger's arrest in Old Canch. It seemed, from his account, that my friend's old charm and bravery had reasserted itself during his arrest. When Maitland poked his head into the under-stairs cupboard, Tiger had said, 'I say old chap, do you have any smokes?' When they clapped the handcuffs on him he gaily apologised that he hadn't washed his wrists for days and would surely get the cuffs dirty. When they closed the back of the horse-drawn Black Maria he played cards with the officer inside, all the way to the city. I assume that Terris had taken a pack of cards with him to Old Canch, to play patience and thus pass some of the time.

As I sipped at my second glass, I told Maitland about my discovery of the ape-man's den, but he just seemed to regard it as an annoying new factor that Romilly had brought into play. 'That Pole won't let anyone in, you know. He won't even answer the door,' Maitland said. He had finished his whisky, and put a very large Packington's Strong Mint in his mouth. It wouldn't do to smell of strong spirits if he encountered another policeman during daylight hours.

'Surely, if you have a warrant you can just go straight into the garden?' I suggested.

'But that's not the object, is it? The idea is to lie in wait for the creature. I'd rather do that in one of the back bedrooms that in the garden, where the ape-man might see us anyway. He might even smell us.'

'Can't you break the door down, if Mochnacki won't open it?' Maitland shook his head. His face was going purple; thanks to his large dose of Scotland's proudest export.

'If the ape-man's anywhere near, the noise will frighten him off,' he said. 'Anyway, we're talking about a very well-built house. Those doors were made for the protection of people who actually have some property to protect. They won't just fall in like the doors in a tenement. I'm not ready to go charging around with a sharpened tree-trunk at my time of life.' I guessed that by this he meant some sort of improvised battering-ram.

'I know how we could get in,' I said, tossing off the last of my whisky.

'How?'

'You say he won't answer the door.'

'Right.'

'Well, he must answer to the messenger boys who bring his food and everything.'

'Yes.'

'Well, if we knock on his door very early in the morning, he might open it, thinking we're his delivery boys. And if I'm there, he might not slam the door shut again. He knows me. I recently made a portrait of him.'

Chapter XVIII

That evening, the papers were full of the arrest of Allan Terris, for the murder of Esau Harrison. He had been taken very quickly to a remand cell in Durham Gaol. The idea that, just a few minutes' walk away from my house, my friend was lying in prison, was very difficult. Worse, I couldn't visit the man or send him anything to comfort him. And it had been my folly, in bringing his pipe into Durham to be repaired, that had put him in prison. I could so easily have bought him a new pipe and told the tobacconist that it was for myself!

The photography shop was quiet, and I sat and had a mid-morning cup of tea with Hebe.

'The evidence against our friend Tiger is pretty damning,' I remarked. By this time I assumed that, in a conversation with her father, she had learned everything about Tiger, and myself, and Old Canch.

'The fact that he ran away doesn't help,' she said, drifting over to the shop window with her tea, and looking out. 'Do you realise, Jacob, that by helping your friend you might have lost this shop, and me, and more than you could have imagined? In fact, that could still happen, if the tobacconist, or Tiger himself, or any of the police let slip that you helped a fugitive.'

'I thought your father had squared all that,' I said.

'Squared it? He's ready to perjure himself in court and risk his job for you. For us. But you could still end up in prison. My father's never done any of this 'squaring' before. He's the straightest copper on the Durham force.'

'If I get locked up,' I asked, 'will you wait for me?' Hebe had brought me down to earth with a bump, and I suddenly felt very bruised and tired.

'The question is not ''will I wait for you''. The question is, whether you survive being locked up! I sit in this shop every day, and I see hearses going to and from the prison up the road all the time. My father tells me they die of despair, or they're worn out by hard labour: turning handles, breaking up rocks, walking on treadmills... And a lot of the prisoners go mad, and end up at Winterton, or Backram's.'

'I'm helping your father with Mochnacki tomorrow morning. And I've not been involved in any crimes before. Surely these things will count in my favour?' I put in. Probably I should have said, 'I've never been *arrested* for any crimes before'. My youthful involvement with the attempt to steal from Mr Broadlock weighed heavily on my mind in those days. Although it was a long way in the past, it had always been my most vivid memory, until the events surrounding the death of Esau Harrison.

Hebe was standing silhouetted against the shop window. She had an excellent figure. That day, she wasn't even wearing her customary corset, yet she still had the fashionable hourglass shape.

'I know he's your friend, Jacob,' she said, 'but he might actually be a murderer.'

'What if Tiger is found to be innocent?' I asked her. There was a pause.

'I don't know what happens then. I'm only a policeman's daughter…'

'But I would have been helping an innocent man.'

'Everyone's innocent until proved guilty, in English law, Jacob.'

'I know, but…'

'The police just wanted to arrest Tiger. They haven't proved him guilty, even now. The police don't even punish the criminals. They just catch them. You helped to stop them doing that.'

Not surprisingly, a silence came into the shop at that moment, and we were both preoccupied with our fears for the future. Prison. Disgrace.

The next morning was very fine, and I went with Inspector Maitland to the house of the reclusive Pole, Mochnacki.

From the front, the house looked well, but very neglected. It had a front garden, but this was almost as overgrown as the back. Because delivery boys came to drop off orders here, the path up the middle of the garden was reasonably clear. The rest was in such a sorry state that I estimated that four strong men would need to work for a summer's day to even begin to establish order.

The butcher's boy and his bike passed us as we neared the gate. Maitland and I tried to look as if we just happened to be standing in that part of the street, and had no interest in Mochnacki's house. While we watched from the start of the garden path, the boy knocked with a distinctive knock, which was obviously a code. The Pole opened the door so quickly that he must have been waiting just behind it. He took something wrapped in paper from the boy, and then closed the door.

The boy cycled off past the post-box at the end of the street. We approached the door and I used the coded knock I'd memorised from when the boy had used it. The pale, sensitive face of Mochnacki appeared almost immediately.

'Mr Mochnacki,' I said, before he could draw his head in again. 'I'm the photographer, Jacob Blount. Do you remember me? I've brought my father-in-law Inspector Maitland with me.'

'Police?' asked the Pole, placing the stress on the first syllable.

Maitland was standing behind me, looking as jolly and harmless as possible under the circumstances. 'We think you may be in danger,' I added. Mochnacki's face fell into a mask of annoyance and reluctance. He opened his door wider and gestured to us to come in.

Inside Mochnacki's hallway, there was a small carver chair with a pile of paper wrappers under it, resting on a silver tray. Clearly, Mochnacki sat here early in the mornings, ready to collect his daily supplies of food, drink, tobacco and newspapers. We followed him as he carried the tray and its burden to the foot of the kitchen stairs. 'Wait there please,' he said, without turning his head. He descended into the obscurity of the underground kitchen. He was dressed in a soiled dressing gown worn on top of a waistcoat and a large, floppy tie. He looked like an older, dirtier version of the Aesthetic student, Sekt. Like Esau Harrison, he wore an embroidered smoking-hat with a tassel. He had clearly not shaved yet. His house was just as clogged with dust and soot as it had been when I'd taken his picture. The idea of living alone in such a large house without servants seemed quite inconceivable to me. Presumably, the man was cooking for himself and even doing his own laundry, occasionally.

Maitland and I wandered over to the entrance of what must once have been a rather grand study. There was a large oil-painting of Mochnacki's uncle over the fire-place. As a photographer, I would have called the picture seriously under-exposed. In truth, the soot from many years of fires had coated the varnish, so that the Little Count appeared to be wandering in an abyss of darkness. There was a velvet pelmet about the fire, and a thick door-curtain hooked up above our heads. Both of these appeared to be black, but may have been any colour: they were simply packed with dust and soot. The windows were so caked with soot that they reminded me of a house gutted by fire. The furniture seemed to be the same as it had been in the Count's time, and it included an easy chair, a dining chair and a table that had been made to the Count's dimensions. A very small child could have been comfortable in these, but it was obvious that even little Mochnicki could not have used them without breaking them or falling over.

Mochnicki was in the room with us before we realised that he was even coming in. He appeared pale and very troubled, and edged behind a sofa in the corner. He did not, however, look particularly old. Not for the first time, I was surprised that a man born when the Little Count was born, in the eighteenth century, could have had a nephew of this age. I was forced to remember that Count Joseph Boruwlaski was not the last of his parents' children to be born. Mochnicki was probably a late child born to one of the Count's younger sisters (since he did not bear the name Boruwlaski). We waited for Mochnicki to invite us to sit down, but he did not.

'Count, I...' my father-in-law began.

'I do not have the honour of being a Count of any kind,' Mochnacki said. 'It was my uncle who claimed that title.'

'Well,' said Maitland, 'I thought that if you'd inherited his money and his house, you would also inherit his title...'

'I did not think it would be appropriate for a Jew to inherit his title.'

'I see. Well, Mr Mochnicki. I'm sorry to have disturbed your morning. I'll get straight to the point. Are you aware that a sort of tramper or derelict has been camping out in your garden? Your back garden, I mean, that slopes down to the river?'

'No, I did not know that,' said Mochnacki, pulling his arms around his ribs. 'Who is he?' The Pole's look of alarm intensified into a look of creeping terror.

'We have no idea of his name,' said Maitland, 'but we think he may be connected to a number of thefts that have recently happened near the river.'

'Oh dear,' said the Pole, looking about, as if the tramp might be hiding somewhere in the room.

'Have you been burgled lately?' Maitland asked.

'No. Not that I know of.' Mochnacki was shivering now.

'Do you ever go out in that garden, sir?'

'No. Never. Is this man out there at the moment?'

'I don't know, sir. Could we take a look?' asked Maitland, readying himself to go outside.

The Pole started to lead us out of the door to the garden, but the Inspector cut him off. 'If we could look from an upstairs window, sir, we could avoid trampling over the man's little nest. That would arouse his suspicions, of course, if he noticed our footprints.' Mochnacki turned around and looked up at my father-in-law.

'So you want to lie in wait for him, Inspector?' he asked. He seemed to be concerned for the man's safety.

'We won't have to if he's here now,' said Maitland, drifting across to the foot of the stairs. 'But don't feel sorry for him, sir. We know him to be capable of violence. He's not worth protecting.' Mochnacki led us upstairs.

In one of the back bedrooms, Maitland quietly pulled open a sash window, unhooked one of the external wooden blinds and opened it just a crack. I looked through after he had done a quick survey. By moving my head to and fro I could see most of the garden. There was no sign of anyone, ape-man or otherwise, but the part of the garden that contained the glass-house was invisible behind the bushes, even from this far up. I was pleased to see that I had left no obvious sign when I had ventured into the garden myself. The only thing that seemed out of place in the garden was a tin tray. The tray was a yard or so from the back door, and held a large enamel jug, a cup and a dinner-plate. Maitland turned to speak to me.

'Assuming that he can't find his way at night, and that he'll be much more visible in the day, I'd guess that our man will come here at dusk, if he comes at all today.' Having established his observation post, Maitland put on his hat. 'Jacob, I will meet you outside the front of this house at eight o'clock tonight, and we'll do a crepuscular watch. That is, if Mr Mochnicki allows?' The Pole was standing by the door, the top half of his body slanted forward in a gesture of panicked gratitude.

'Oh yes. I don't want a stranger sleeping in my garden!' he said.

As we walked back down the street, I asked Maitland, 'You saw the tray, didn't you?'

'I did.'

'So I'm not the only one who helps fugitives,' I said, rather sticking my neck out.

'The situation here is different,' Maitland said, with suppressed anger. 'We don't know for sure that the man who is camping out in Mochnacki's garden is the same man who is stealing from people around the river. And in any case, the Pole may not have known until now that the police wanted to know more about the man – if he is a man.'

'But he does get the newspapers,' I said, referring to Mochnacki.

'That's no proof that he reads them,' said Maitland. 'Some people just use them to light fires, or to wrap up their rubbish. He may only read the national news and any snippets about Poland. He might avoid news about local crimes altogether.'

'I suppose there's no crime against feeding

somebody who happens to live in your garden?'

'None that I know of,' Maitland assured me.

'But why would he help a complete stranger who was hiding in his garden?'

'Why did you help a suspected murderer?'

'He is my friend, as you well know, Maitland,' I said in a low voice.

'My mam always used to say to me that I should try to be friends with everybody,' said Maitland.

That evening, Mochnicki was ready for us with a silver tray full of tea things, and two plates of chicken sandwiches. Although he'd just had dinner at my house, Maitland stuffed half the sandwiches into his pockets and took up his post at the window he had chosen. 'Romilly doesn't eat,' he explained, referring to the sergeant, who was posted in a corner of the garden itself, at the end nearest the river.

The plan was that I would watch from the upstairs window. If and when the ape-man landed on the ground inside the garden, I would whistle, and Maitland would rush downstairs. The two detectives would put handcuffs on the ape-man. As a civilian, I was not supposed to go near their captive. Maitland did not feel up to the task of watching for the man, as his eyesight was not particularly good. Despite the protestations of his daughter, he refused to wear glasses, as he thought they would make him look old and scholarly.

While I was watching, Maitland would be sitting on the stairs, ostensibly guarding Mochnacki. In fact, he was making sure that the Pole did not try to warn the ape-man of our presence.

Very quickly, the sun was peeping through the riverside trees and the evening chorus of the birds was fading away. I felt cold and uncomfortable sitting on an ornate bedroom chair, straining my neck to see through the gap in the shutters. I was soon a little hungry, and wished I had pocketed some of Mochnicki's sandwiches. It was easy to see the whole garden in the half-light, because my eyes had had plenty of time to become accustomed to it. I could see Sergeant Romilly's narrow figure leaning, immobile and soundless, against the corner of the garden wall. His right hand was thrust deep into his trouser pocket. His left was tucked into an opening in his waistcoat. A little Napoleon, I thought.

The first thing that I saw coming over the wall was an amorphous, dark shape that didn't climb over at all – it flew right over without touching the wall and landed in a heap. I gasped. This was not what I had expected. This object was quickly followed by a large, floppy hat, not connected to any kind of head. The hat landed on the previous object and bounced into a bush. It was obvious that Romilly had seen these things: he assumed the position of a man about to start a running race over medium distance. In his hand he held a truncheon which he must have had concealed somewhere in his clothes. He glanced up to where I was, presumably to check I had seen what he had seen.

It was only after the hat landed that a pair of very dark hands grasped the top of the wall; the right first, and then the left. At first I assumed that the hands wore dark gloves, but when the head emerged I changed my mind.

The creature that climbed over the wall wore a pair of baggy black trousers held up with braces. Under the braces he had a grey collarless shirt. He wore heavy workmen's boots, which did not, however, impede his climbing ability at all. He dropped down onto the grass and weeds on my side of the garden wall and dusted itself off: the wall had deposited a lot of dry stone dust on the trousers, giving the creature the appearance of a stonemason. As he looked around for his hat, and what I now surmised was a coat, he saw Romilly with his truncheon.

The pair observed each other with mutual surprise. The sergeant's usual dry, cynical face had opened into an expression of utter shock. I whistled loudly through my fingers, then felt the shaking of the whole house as Maitland thundered down the stairs. Soon the Inspector was charging out of the house. His progress across the overgrown lawn was somewhat impeded by the fact that Mochnacki was on his back, hanging with his hands clasped around Maitland's neck.

As if unaware of the dangling Pole, Maitland seized the ape-man with one hand and fumbled for his own truncheon with the other. The creature twisted and kicked him while Romilly approached and thumped the ape-man on the head. The creature's head dropped down for a second, and he staggered, but he seemed to shake off the blow. The bump on my own head seemed to tingle when I saw this.

Romilly threw his truncheon aside and tried to hook his arms up around the creature's shoulders. The ape-man, trapped by this grip, which we English call a Full Nelson, fought it in the only way possible: he kicked the shins of the man who had hold of him. Since he was wearing such hard, heavy boots Romilly was soon in great pain. As he slipped out of the Full Nelson, the ape-man started to pummel the Inspector's face with his free hand. By this time my very well-fed father-in-law was out of breath and the ape-man was able to twist out of his grip.

Out of some mad wish to please Maitland, I decided to join the fray at this point. I had been told not to get close to the fugitive if he should come into the garden, but I felt a sense of obligation to Maitland, and a desire to earn his trust. I noticed that the ape-man, in his struggles, was trying to make towards the house, and more specifically the back door, which was open.

He would of course have been foolish to head for the wall, since to climb up would merely have invited the detectives to pull at his legs. No. The back door offered a real possibility of escape, especially since, in most British houses, the front door is easy to open from the inside. He was probably planning to rush through the whole ground floor of the house.

A thick tangle of briars between Mochnacki's house and his side-fence meant that there was no way round the side of the house.

Believing that the creature would try for the back door, I positioned myself inside it, out of sight. As the ape-man rushed through, I extended my leg and tripped him over. I had expected to delay him by this manoeuvre, or perhaps to direct his anger toward myself. Instead, much to my surprise, he went down and stayed down. The two detectives stood at the door and regarded the immobile body.

'Looks like your feeble truncheon-work finally took effect, Romilly,' said my father-in-law. From outside, I heard the sound of Mochnacki's sobbing. He had dropped off Maitland's back at the climax of the fight, and was now mourning the loss of his friend.

Chapter XIX

I did not accompany the policemen and their captive to the station, but I later heard the details of everything that had happened there from my father-in-law.

Some hours after he had fallen unconscious, the Durham ape-man woke up in a cell under the City Police Station. By this time, he had been stripped and thoroughly examined by Dr Terris, in the presence of no less than seven police officers, of both the uniformed and private clothes persuasions. Most of these policemen did not need to be there, but all of them were fairly boggling with curiosity. The examination was carried out in the creature's locked cell, for fear that it might escape. He lay unconscious on a trestle table that had been brought in specially for the purpose of the examination. An electric bulb inside a little cage in the ceiling of the cell provided all the illumination.

Dr Terris worked quickly: he knew that with

nine people breathing it, the air of the cell could not remain healthy for long. He was also disturbed in his work by the unusual smell of the creature itself. It was not an entirely unpleasant smell, but it was certainly unusual.

Dr Terris found that the ape-man was covered with thick black fur, rather than hair. It was like the fur of a black Newfoundland dog, when it has just been clipped in spring. The skin underneath the fur was pink. When Dr Terris lifted up the eyelids of the insensible creature, the irises proved to be brown – the commonest colour among humans. The general proportions and attitudes of the limbs looked human, at least on superficial observation, although the knees were reluctant to straighten out, and the creature was bow-legged. This bow-leggedness, usually caused by rickets, is called 'the English disease' by some. It is thought to be caused by our poor diet, which can make for a tragic softness of the bones in infancy.

The fingernails of the creature were much roughened and eroded, and very dirty, but they were obviously human. The teeth, which Dr Terris examined with great caution, were found to be dirty and neglected but of quite normal human size and shape. The doctor felt the back of the skull, where Romilly's truncheon had struck. When the creature started to groan, Terris stood back and told the policemen to hold the prisoner down.

When he was safely outside of the locked cell, the doctor declared, 'He has a slight concussion. He may have a headache for a while.'

'The creature is obviously a lunatic escaped from a nearby asylum,' Terris opined as he drank tea with the Inspector, in the latter's office. 'I would send a couple of detectives up to Winterton straight away if I were you, Maitland. If they claim that they haven't mislaid a dangerous idiot, you just ask your men to look at their records. Hotels, hospitals, asylums – they all have to record arrivals and departures. Their incomes depend on it.'

'His skull looked pretty large to me, Doctor,' said Maitland, tentatively suggesting a medical observation to the respected doctor. 'Are you sure he's as idiot?'

'The skull doesn't really reflect what's inside it, Inspector. That is a fallacy of the phrenologists. You're not a bump-feeler are you?' asked the doctor, referring to the then popular pseudo-science of phrenology.

'No no,' the Inspector insisted, probably to avoid the scorn of the medical man. 'It's just that I've heard something about these idiots with the tiny skulls...' Dr Terris smiled at him condescendingly.

'One could envisage a microcephalic idiot with an enlarged skull due to hydrocephalus,' he explained. 'Of course, he would be an individual with a peculiarly unlucky medical history. A tiny brain trapped inside a huge skull full of fluid? It hardly bears thinking about. The feeble function of his brain would be further impeded by the build-up of fluid. In effect, his intellect, such as it was, would be constantly drowning.'

'I think you're talking about water on the brain, Doctor?' Maitland ventured. The doctor nodded.

'What about all the hair?' Maitland asked.

'Oh, it has been observed, by Mr Darwin among others, that idiots are often rather hairy. Indeed, hairiness is a trait that civilised humans like us instinctively associate with lack of intelligence and lack of civilisation. Think of the savages of Africa and South America, for instance. They hunt in the forest and wantonly procreate, but do they have architecture? Do they follow a revealed religion? Can they be said to possess anything approaching science? I have never heard of those unfortunate individuals visiting a barber. Have you, Inspector?'

'Visited a barber?' asked Maitland, somewhat puzzled. 'Oh, you mean the savages? Well, no. I suppose not.'

Maitland fell silent. As he told me afterwards, he had seen engraved photographs of savages from all over the world, but he had never seen a human with so much hair as the ape-man, then groaning in the cell beneath his feet.

'Will you come back tomorrow to visit our savage, Dr Terris?' Maitland asked, when the doctor stood up and started to put on his gloves.

'I must decline that invitation, Inspector,' the physician replied.

'May I ask why, sir?'

'I trained to cure the sick among the human race, in Britain. I do not wish to assume the duties of an animal doctor, an alienist or a medical missionary. Good night, Inspector Maitland.'

Chapter XX

The creature was charged with several thefts in the city, as well as an assault attempted on the young serving-girl. A Black Maria, pulled by two horses, took him on the short journey to Durham Gaol, where he was to become a remand prisoner. At this time he was apparently conscious and alert, but he hadn't uttered a sound except for groaning.

A solicitor was picked out for him, and a barrister was chosen to act as his defence counsel. The latter was a young fellow called Harburton. I would know little about Harburton's dealings with the ape-man, were it not for the fact that the barrister was a member of the celebrated Chemical Club of Durham.

Harburton had an interest in forensic science. He used his knowledge of this comparatively new field to puzzle witnesses, and expert witnesses, when defending criminal cases. He had more than earned his stripes as a member of the Chemical Club when he caused the acquittal of a gamekeeper on a charge of attempted murder. He questioned the witnesses in such a way that it became obvious that the gamekeeper could not have fired the bullet that nearly killed the intended victim.

The gamekeeper, an acknowledged expert on rifles, would not have stored his ammunition so poorly that it was nearly dead when he fired it. The bullet in question, Harburton argued in his summing-up, had been so damp that it had practically crawled out of the barrel, and bounced feebly off the bones of the victim's skull.

Thanks to his membership of the Chemical Club, Harburton felt able to fill me in on the details of the case as he saw it, while the case was in progress. As we sat in a corner of the Half-Moon, at the end of a particularly arduous meeting of the Chemical Club of Durham, he told me of his feelings of bewilderment regarding his client.

'Imagine how I must feel,' he said, 'after just a few years at the bar, bringing an ape into the Court.'

'Yes Harburton,' I agreed, 'it must be among the most bizarre spectacles ever presented before the bench in Durham.'

'Of course,' he said, 'animals used to be quite seriously tried in the law courts of the

Middle Ages.'

'Really?'

'Oh yes. In York, a pig was tried for committing adultery.'

'How could a pig commit adultery?' I asked, agog. Harburton drank a small point of order.

'Why, by lying with the wife of the farmer!' he explained.

'I see!'

'It seems that the poor woman had recently given birth to a peculiarly ugly baby. The unfortunate infant looked like a pig.'

'What was the outcome of the case?' I asked.

'Can't remember,' said the barrister. 'And I'm sure you will recall, Blount,' he went on, 'how the good people of Hartlepool hanged a monkey in the belief that it was a French spy.'

'Ah yes,' I said. 'Hartlepudlians are known to this day as 'Monkey-hangers'. This is something I learned shortly after I came to live in this county.'

When Harburton returned to the case of the ape-man, his tone became somewhat more serious.

'My nightmare client may or may not be human: opinions differ on that point. I am at present unsure as to whether he can speak in any human language, let alone English. My client seems to have no name and, since he never speaks, the business of finding out exactly who he is problematic. I cannot discuss his case with him. Yesterday, he would not plead either guilty or not guilty to his various thefts.

'At the most, the sentence for his petty thefts might be a few years in prison, at hard labour. The punishment might be more severe if the defendant appeared to be some kind of dumb savage. The judge might feel that he should be put behind bars, just to protect the public.' Harburton shook his head and assumed another point of order.

'If he would speak, I think the court might see him as human and act humanely towards him. I had the idea of getting a doctor to examine my client's throat and mouth, to see if he is physically able to speak. I wasted some time sending for Doctor Terris, who had of course already decided that the ape-man was not human, and should not be treated by a physician like himself. He also implied that the creature could not be tried in a normal court of law, being an animal, or at least sub-human. Terris sent my messenger round to Dr Codling.'

'Did Codling come?'

'Indeed he did. He went up the beast's cell with me.' I smiled inwardly at this. I could only imagine the stir that this effete, overdressed, overfed young doctor had on the other inmates as he passed along the ape-man's landing. I do not think for one minute that Codling toned down his flamboyant necktie to suit the sombre grey of the prison.

Durham Gaol was at that time given over to a version of the old Separate System of incarceration, whereby convicts were kept alone, and saw little if anything of their fellow-inmates. As a remand prisoner, the creature was theoretically presumed innocent under British law, and had nothing to do but to learn the habits of idleness.

'Codling was not in the least taken aback by my client's appearance,' Harburton told me. 'The only furniture in the room was the wooden pallet where my client lay, staring at the ceiling. Codling, quite out of breath from his walk up the iron stairs, squeezed himself onto this primitive bed.

'I explained to the creature that Dr Codling was a physician, and that he had come to find out if he, my client, could talk.

'Now, Codling surprised me then. He said that he already knew that the creature *could* speak. He said he'd learned about Dr Terris's experience of our hairy friend. Terris mentioned that my client groaned quite distinctly when he woke up in the police station.

"Now, groaning is vocalisation," said Codling. "It means that you have a voice, sir. And according to the warden for this landing, you talk very distinctly in your sleep."

My client sat up and put a hairy hand to the side of his hairy face, all the time gazing intently at the doctor.

"Sleep-talking is a terrible menace for people who pretend to be dumb, for whatever reason," Codling went on. "I suppose that to keep the secret one should sleep alone in a soundproof room. At the moment, you are forced to sleep with several hundreds of other men, all the time watched over by attentive wardens. Now, although the walls are good and thick, the doors here are made of iron and they transmit sound very well."

At this, the ape-man closed his eyes.

"If Dr Codling is right," I said to my client, "then you really must talk to me, and later you must speak out in court."

The ape-man coughed, then asked, "What did I say in my sleep?"'

After their interview with the ape-man, Harburton and Codling headed for the Court Inn, the local lawyers' public house. I can imagine that in that unbuttoned, masculine atmosphere, some incredulous faces might have been turned to Codling in his immaculate dove-grey suit. The place seemed to be designed for secluded little conferences, and the two men quickly found an empty booth in a dark corner.

'It is Hypertrichosis, otherwise known as hirsutism,' said Codling. 'The bearded ladies in circuses are an example of the same condition. You may also have heard of the hairy family of Siam. I've seen a photograph of them. They became such favourites at the court of the King of Siam that the King paid a man to marry one of the daughters. It strikes me that this treatment was rather better than what we British have done to the Durham ape-man: making him a circus freak.'

'Then it's hereditary?' Harburton asked, starting his brandy and soda.

'It can be, yes,' said the doctor. 'Of course, physicians have looked for symptoms other than excessive hairiness in these cases, but the condition is too rare for any really systematic data to be obtainable.'

'One hears stories of hairy wild men in jungles and forests all over the world. Could these be families of men like our friend Isaac, who have hidden themselves away for shame?' Just after he had asked about his own sleep-talking, the hairy man had given Harburton and Codling his name.

'I've never thought of it, Harburton, but I suppose it might be true. Funny he should be called Isaac, though.'

'How do you mean?'

'Well, Isaac in the Bible had two sons who fell out over his inheritance,' Codling explained. 'Esau was the hairy one who hunted down the family's meat. Jacob was the smooth one who looked after the domesticated animals. Isaac preferred Esau, but Jacob got the inheritance by subterfuge. Don't you know all this?'

'I think I must have forgotten it. From the point of view of a lawyer, it sounds like an interesting case of a contested will. I suppose Isaac's surname, Batey, doesn't appear in the Bible?'

'I'd have to check in Cruden's Concordance, but I'm pretty sure it doesn't.'

They both laughed, and Harburton bought more drinks. Although the two young men had only just met, they were getting along famously, helped by the fact of their mutual interest in the ape-man.

'What line of defence will you take now, Harburton?' the doctor asked.

'I think I'll play down the fact that Batey came from a circus. The sort of men who end up on juries in Durham may not be the sort to appreciate such low forms of entertainment.'

'Won't you want to point up the fact that he felt humiliated there, being looked at and commented on all the time by the public?'

'I'm not sure about that. Some of the jurors might have seen similar exhibits in the past. It might not do to make them feel guilty. No. I think the best I can do is to play down the assault charge, on the basis of the girl's not having had any injuries. I mean the girl whose basket he snatched, of course. If I call her as a witness, her undoubted brawniness might count in my favour. It may be that I can cast some doubt on her character by interviewing her mistress – that is, if I can get that lady to appear in court. Otherwise, the direct evidence linking Isaac to any of the other thefts around the river is slight.'

'Wasn't he seen by a student?'

'Yes, but a short-sighted student who didn't have his glasses on at the time. The youth is, from what I can gather, a curiously unimpressive example of studious manhood. The fact that he failed to try and apprehend the robber will surely count against him.'

'What about the old man who saw him? Billy something.'

'Old Billy Robson saw him, and got a good look at him; but Isaac Batey wasn't committing a crime at that moment. Swimming in the river isn't a crime, you know. Taking one's clothes off to swim can be an offence, but this ape-man can never really be naked, can he? That is, unless he plies his razor for many hours on end!'

'Will you try to contact the circus he deserted?'

'I don't think so. The gentlemen of the Durham jury will not take to the idea of a clown or a juggler being hauled in as a character witness.'

Outside the Court Inn, the two new friends parted company with a warm handshake.

'By the way,' said Harburton, turning back. 'When did you talk to that warder about Batey's sleep-talking?'

'I didn't,' said Codling. 'Call it a legal fiction.'

Chapter XXI

By the time Tiger Terris came to trial, I had not seen him at all for some time. When the trial started, Adah Harrison was still judged unfit to testify. She continued in the care of Mrs Roberson at her flat. Some of the erstwhile devotees of Esau Harrison now contributed money to her welfare. It seems that they now viewed their late master as a great loss to the world. The large sums of cash found in the flat had been impounded by the crown as evidence. Adah could not use any of that money as yet.

Looking round the courtroom, which was packed to the rafters, I saw Dr Terris sitting a few yards away from me in the public seats. He looked pale and drawn, and much older than he had looked when I had seen him last. He looked as if he hadn't been eating at all for many days. I also saw the barrister, Mr Harburton, who would later be continuing the case for the defence of the Durham ape-man, now known as Isaac Batey. The papers of the time informed me that the Tiger Terris case was Harburton's first murder case. As far as I could see across the packed courtroom, Harburton was sweaty and nervous under his 'cauliflower' wig. I would certainly have been nervous in his position.

If Harburton did not keep his wits about him, Terris might hang. Later in the same court, if his defence of Isaac Batey failed, that defendant might spend years at hard labour. Harburton kept turning nervously to the solicitor who was there to support him, a very ancient looking legal type called Edgeley who looked as if he had just been retrieved from a dusty cupboard at their chambers. Given the evident decrepitude of his assistant, it was easy to see why Harburton had taken such at active part in preparing his current cases. He was never the type of barrister to restrict his contribution entirely to the courtroom. In this he resembled the legendary Edward Marshall Hall, the Henry Irving of the English Bar.

The first witnesses in the trial were all people who were directly involved in events surrounding the discovery of the body of Esau Harrison. These included Mrs Roberson, who again appeared in a very fetching 'picture' hat. She turned her fine profile to the men of the jury; a jury that she knew was partly made up of bachelors and widowers of about her age. Mrs

Roberson's daughter Alice was also questioned. In other words, we all witnessed a repetition of the evidence at the Coroner's Inquest.

Dr Codling, who had examined the body of Esau Harrison, was questioned at length by the counsels for the prosecution and for the defence. Harburton, as counsel for the defence, was very keen to bring out one particular point towards the end of his questioning of this expert medical witness:

'No, I cannot give any conclusive judgement as to how or why Mr Harrison died,' Codling replied to a particularly pertinent question from his new friend.

'But at the Inquest you said that belladonna poisoning was the cause.'

'I did, but I now believe that Mr Harrison probably didn't take enough of that poison to kill him.'

'And why did you change your mind?'

'Two reasons, really. First, the bottle of belladonna was found in the bathroom of the deceased, not by the chair where he was found dead.' At this, counsel for the prosecution raised an objection: Dr Codling was commenting on non-medical aspects of the case. The judge testily overruled the objection. Codling was commenting on the physical position of a substance of medical interest, and medicine was his field of expertise. The prosecutor sat down with a great show of annoyance.

'And your second reason?' Harburton asked.

'There was enough belladonna missing from the bottle to kill a man of Mr Harrison's age and size, but not to kill him quickly.'

'What does that signify?'

'Well, unless a very large dose is taken *very quickly*, belladonna poisoning is accompanied by convulsive movements of the body. According to Mr Jacob Blount's excellent photograph of the body *in situ*, there were no signs of any such convulsions. Harrison was sitting upright in a fireside chair, very comfortably.'

'Couldn't he have restrained his convulsions, assuming that he suffered any, by sheer willpower?'

Codling answered no to this ghoulish question. 'Under an onslaught from such a substance, the body will convulse itself. Willpower doesn't really apply here.'

'So, if you are ruling out poisoning with belladonna, how do you think the man died?

'I don't know.'

'Is there anything in your findings to suggest that Mr Harrison might not have killed himself, Dr Codling?'

'Absolutely nothing at all. In fact, I think there is a large chance that he did kill himself, and was not murdered at all.'

'Thank you, Dr Codling.'

Harburton had found the main breach in the earthworks of the prosecution. If it was not clear how Harrison was murdered, or even *if* he was murdered, the jury might hesitate to send Tiger Terris, the supposed murderer, to the scaffold. The counsel for the prosecution, still red in the face after his objection had been overruled, stood up to question Dr Codling.

'Although you appear to be a comparatively young man, Dr Codling, I understand that you have provided evidence at a number of Inquests and trials, and that you are often called to perform autopsies where the cause of death is doubtful. Is this true?'

'I suppose so.'

'Among the murders you have investigated, in a medical way,' counsel for the prosecution resumed, 'what percentage of those victims were killed by people who were then living in, or had lived in, the victim's own place of abode?'

'Quite a high percentage, I should think.'

'It's actually eighty percent, Dr Codling. That's the percentage for the murders you have investigated. I was able to work out the percentage without too much trouble,' said the prosecutor, waggishly, 'as you have carried out autopsies on five people so far in your career. That is, five people who have subsequently been found to have been murder victims. Of those only one was killed by a stranger, and one other was killed by her husband, who had not lived with her for years.' Harburton began to stand up.

'Before my learned friend raises any objection,' the prosecution continued, 'I would like to add that it is generally known that we all have more chance of being murdered by someone we live with than by anyone else.'

'Objection, your honour,' said Harburton, wearily. 'We are here to try this case on the facts, not on a set of statistics.' The judge allowed the objection.

The accused, Tiger Terris, appeared at the start of the next day in the crown court. Whereas his father was growing lean and desperate with worry about the case, Tiger had somehow managed to wax large on prison food. But it was not the jolly fatness of the free man: the pallor of the prison was upon Terris, and the beard he had grown at Old Canch remained to cover the lower half of his face. Above this wall of black, his eyes seemed to peep out fearfully, like the eyes of a cat, hiding behind a bush.

As was customary, Harburton had had one of the accused's suits brought in for him, so that he would not have to wear prison clothes in the dock. Someone, perhaps Mrs Roberson, had picked a sober black one from among Tiger's clothes: this was mated with a dark blue necktie and a white shirt. Unfortunately, both shirt and suit were now too small for Tiger. The front of his waistcoat had a sadly corrugated appearance, and his neck bulged sideways over his shirt collar.

He looked around the court with a disillusioned eye. He did not appear to recognise anyone. It is possible that friends in the court who had not seen his full beard were finding it hard to recognise him. At times he seemed to sway in his place. The longer he stood, the more his shoulders slid down, so that, in a macabre way, he sometimes looked as though he were hanging already.

Counsel for the prosecution, having been somewhat blunted on the previous day, returned to the attack like a freshly sharpened knife.

'Captain Terris, why did you decide to move out of your father's house into the home of Mr and Mrs Harrison?' he asked. Tiger shrugged.

'I had argued with my father,' he said, faintly. 'I had made friends with Esau. They had a spare room...'

'What did you argue with your father about?'

'He didn't like the hours I was keeping. He thought I was drinking too much. He was treating me like a child, really. I've been in the army, out in India, you know. I was a captain. I couldn't accept the discipline of the old *paterfamilias* any more.' At these words, Dr Terris looked down at his own feet.

'Do you believe that you really were drinking to excess at this time?' Tiger shrugged again. I wished he wouldn't shrug. It seemed to imply his vague disrespect for the court.

'I think I was indulging a little too much at that time, yes. They teach you how to drink in the army, you know. I'd got used to a lot of drink out in India.' The prosecutor smiled.

'So I have heard,' like an old stager, the barrister waited until a small rustle of laughter subsided. 'Now, Mr Harrison was a sort of faith healer, was he not?' he resumed.

'Yes.'

'Were you undergoing any sort of cure when you were living with him? One hears of people who go to live with an aunt in the country for a few weeks to ease their bronchitis. Was there anything of that sort going on in Old Elvet?'

'Yes.'

'So, what was being cured?' Tiger sank still

further into his clothes.

'I've always been able to give up drinking whenever duty called,' he answered, 'or when I ran out of money, or after I'd made a fool of myself. But laudanum. Laudanum is a horse of a different colour.' Most of the people in the court seemed to breathe in all at once.

'Laudanum? You were a laudanum addict as well as a toper?' asked the prosecutor.

'Yes.'

'Where did you pick up this habit? Was it in India?'

'No. The opium poppy is grown there, of course. But I never took laudanum in India. I didn't *smoke* any poppy out there, either. I started right here in Durham.' Tiger paused. 'Old Harrison was going to cure me of the laudanum addiction.'

'Really. And how was he going to achieve that?' the prosecutor asked.

'By hypnotism. And by supplying me with smaller and smaller amounts of the drug.'

'And did this work?'

'I don't think I was as susceptible to the hypnotism as some of his subjects. And he was reducing the dosage too quickly, I thought.' Tiger's answers were informative enough, but he continued to deliver them with an air of indifference that cannot have put the jury on his side. The prosecution resumed its questioning.

'Could you have got any laudanum from anyone other than Harrison?'

'Yes, in theory.'

'You say in theory. What happened in practice?'

'In practice he got to all the pharmacists in the city. He warned them not to sell me any opiates.'

'How did you feel about that?'

'I was furious. One comes to depend on a drug like laudanum. It's very unpleasant to be deprived of it. The doses Harrison was giving me satisfied me for only a few hours. When they wore off, I was cold and miserable, and the pain in my hand came back.'

'Your hand?'

'Yes. That's why I'd started taking laudanum in the first place. As an analgesic. For the pain in my hand.' The prosecution looked disappointed. Tiger had moved onto a subject that was likely win some sympathy for him.

'Your remaining hand is in pain, then?'

'No, that's fine. But I have pain where the other hand should be. It's a phantom pain.'

'Do you have that pain now?' the prosecutor seemed to ask this out of his own compassion and curiosity. It could not possibly help his case to draw attention to Tiger's disfigurement.

'Yes. I have that pain now.' For the first time since he had come into the dock, Tiger stood up straight. A bluff old fellow at the front of the jury flicked a look of admiration at him. He's a hero, the look seemed to say.

'Let us return to the circumstances surrounding the death of Mr Harrison,' said the prosecutor. 'Cast your mind back to before the death of Harrison. You are living with him and his wife in their apartments in Old Elvet. He is regularly hypnotising you and feeding you with smaller and smaller doses of the opiate, laudanum. Did you know where he kept this laudanum?'

'No.'

'Did you search?'

'I practically pulled the place apart one day when both of them were out. I couldn't find anything.'

'And you couldn't get any of the drug from any other source?

'That's right. The pharmacists all knew me.'

'Did you argue with Mr Harrison at this time?'

'Yes. Constantly. He was in a very touchy mood, anyway.'

'Any idea why?'

'I don't know. He threw a couple of newspapers across the room one day, but he wouldn't tell me what was in them to upset him.'

'Would you say that you were irrational, due to the effects of withdrawal from the drug?'

'Yes, I was irrational at times. You see, he sometimes seemed to be lording it over me. It hurt my pride. He seemed to be taunting me.'

'How so?'

'Well, by making me wait until he had finished writing in his journal, before he gave me any laudanum. I know I shouldn't have been annoyed by that. I mean, I knew he wrote his journal for half an hour between half past nine and ten every night, before he went to bed. He even put his pocket-watch on the table while he was writing, so that he wouldn't write for too long. He was a man of very regular habits. But all I knew at that time was, he's not giving me the drug.'

Counsel for the prosecution paused for effect before the next question.

'Mr Terris, did you murder Esau Harrison because you were angry with him about the laudanum?'

'No.'

'Were you the first person to find his body?'

'Possibly. I don't know.'

'No further questions.' The prosecution gathered up his papers and sat down in a swirl of black gown.

Chapter XXII

Outside the courthouse, I ran into my father-in-law, Inspector Maitland.

'What did you think of my friend's performance in the dock?' I asked as we cut down into New Elvet.

'I've certainly seen worse,' he remarked. 'I think your friend Tiger decided to stick by the oath as if it were his dearest mistress.'

'Yes,' I agreed. 'The truth, the whole truth and nothing but the truth.'

'Now the jury knows he took laudanum and that he was driven mad by the lack of it. ' said Maitland, bowling along toward the police station.

'Yes' I agreed.

'I suppose he's never been in court before, and he's probably not been inside a prison before either. An experienced criminal would have been a bit more selective in what he said. An experienced man might even have thought to give the impression that he liked Esau Harrison, and was sorry to find him dead.' Maitland leaned on the railings of the police station and produced a silver-plated cigarette case.

'The prosecutor didn't ask him about why he ran away,' I said.

'He didn't need to,' said Maitland, lighting up with a red-tipped match. 'He was on such a rich seam of testimony about the laudanum and Tiger's anger that he probably wanted to stop when he'd made the point. That silk's an old hand. He knows when to stop, before the defendant changes his mind and tries to muddy the waters. No point boring the jury anyway, especially when it's nearly lunchtime.'

'Do you think the jury will take pity on Tiger because of his hand?'

'Works two ways, something like that,' said my father-in-law, puffing away. 'Some might feel sorry for him, but some might think his disfigurement has driven him to evil.'

Maitland dined inside the station, while I nipped into a bakery for a meat pie. After lunch, Mr Harburton went over much of the same ground as his learned opponent, the judge having given his permission for the defence to cross-examine the accused. Tiger answered as truthfully as he had before, I think out of a sort of resigned despair.

I saw Maitland from a distance outside the courtroom that afternoon, when the court was finally adjourned for the day. I tried to attract his attention, but Romilly appeared and drew him off. I consoled myself a little with the fact that Maitland was due to have dinner with Hebe and myself that night.

Instead of his usual wine or beer, Maitland brought a bottle of whisky this time. He explained that it wasn't for a celebration: we were, in effect, drinking at a wake. His way of putting it was rather harsh and hopeless, but it was entirely accurate. There seemed to be little hope for our mutual friend, Tiger Terris.

As I watched him work his way steadily through an unusually large dinner, I myself could eat hardly anything. I thought that Maitland had probably seen many such cases, and that they could no longer ruin his appetite.

'I suppose you've heard the latest about Batey?' he asked over the cheese. He knew perfectly well that I hadn't heard anything.

'What's happened?'

'Only escaped, hasn't he?'

'How?' I asked.

'Well, it seems he had been complaining of headaches and double vision, and he appeared to black out several times on the remand wing. The prison governor thought it might have something to do with that little tap on the head he got from Romilly.'

'Ah, yes,' I assented.

'When Batey appeared to slip into a permanent state of unconsciousness, the Governor panicked and sent him to the main Durham Hospital. There he remained for about twenty-four hours, in a private ward. A policeman and a prison guard were set to watch him, but they both fell asleep. When a doctor arrived to examine Batey, the patient had gone and the prison guard couldn't be woken up. The policeman was roused to a sort of half-consciousness and pointed to the enamel mugs on the floor. They both contained the remnants of a mug of cocoa, with a dash of laudanum.'

'So somebody laced their cocoa?'

'So it seems.'

'Who gave it to them?'

'The policeman said it was a nurse. He described her, but none of the nurses who work in that part of the hospital can recall any nurse who looks like that. And then we found that a nurse's uniform had gone missing.'

'Didn't anyone spot him going out? Hebe asked, 'he does look a bit unusual, you know.'

'It seems that this fake nurse wheeled him

out on a trolley, with his face covered up like a dead man. They found the trolley in the wrong place, just by a back door.'

'So there's a big search on?'

'Yes, Hebe my dear. We've got a hundred men combing the city, the fields, watching the roads, the train stations: we've even got four men at Old Canch. But I thought I'd rather spend the evening with you two, eating you out of house and home. One can have too much excitement, you know.' I agreed with my father-in-law. I was looking forward to a time when our picturesque little city would return to its quiet, routine self.

It was a surprisingly warm evening but, as the light started to fade, Hebe closed the windows so as to keep out any moths. 'You'll have to smoke outside,' she said. She couldn't stand anyone smoking with the windows closed.

The night was warm and dry, and I sat with Maitland on the edge of the circular stone horse-trough in the middle of the road where New and Old Elvet cross each other. There was nobody else on the street except for two uniformed policemen. They saluted Maitland, who waved to them in silent acknowledgement.

'I suppose everybody's inside because of the escape?' I asked him.

'Yes. But I don't think Batey will be in the

city. He's not stupid. He's a man, according to young Codling. He'll be setting out across country. He may even be out of the county by now. I'm not concerned about him. It's out of my hands. I'm just worried that they're going to hang your friend Tiger on some very flimsy evidence.'

'It's circumstantial evidence, isn't it? Can they really hang him on that?'

'Men have been hanged on circumstantial evidence before. And women, too. Our old friend Mary Ann Cotton, for instance. She was hanged just up the road in Durham Gaol when there was no direct evidence to link her to any of those murders she committed. And she never confessed to anything, either. Mind you, I don't think anyone around here would tell you she was innocent.'

I sat with Maitland: we were quietly smoking some small cigars he had fished out of his top pocket.

'What did this nurse look like, the one who helped Batey escape?'

'She looked like Adah Harrison, if you must know.'

'Then was it Adah?'

'I went straight round to Mrs Roberson's from the hospital, but Adah was there, as large as life. She was there alone, though, so neither

Mrs Roberson nor Alice could testify to how long she'd been in.'

'But she has no connection to Batey, does she?'

'I suppose not, but there's not many girls around here who look like that.'

The police patrol we had seen earlier appeared again. They came up to Maitland. They were two tall, strong lads in their twenties – in fact they looked quite a credit to the force.

'Any news of the hairy chap?' Maitland asked.

'That's what we were going to ask you, sir,' one of them replied.

'Well, I'm not on duty, Robinson. That's why I'm sharing a cigar with my son-in-law. I have no news about Isaac Batey.'

'Goodnight, sir; Mr Blount' Robinson said, smiling. They carried on round the corner.

Maitland and myself finished our cigars at about the same time and cast the stubs into a storm-drain in the street. As he was turning round to make his way back to my house on the bridge, Maitland froze, and his brow creased. 'Hullo!' he said.

'What is it?' I asked, trying to follow his gaze.

'That house. It's Mrs Roberson's house.'

'What about it?'

'All the lights are off.' This was true. The fact was very much accentuated because all the other houses on the street were seriously lit up.

'Perhaps they've gone out,' I offered, but Maitland was already heading for Mrs Roberson's place.

'Adah told me they'd all be in tonight. They're in every night,' he said.

As we approached the house, we heard a phrase shouted from inside, unmistakably in Mrs Roberson's own voice. 'Where are you, Adah?' she cried, but in such panicked tones that it was clear something was seriously wrong. Maitland banged hard on the door, and the same voice cried, 'Who is it?' Maitland identified himself and the lady shouted, 'Oh! Thank God!' and opened the front door.

Inside, there was still no light to be seen, and another female voice was gibbering, so it seemed, inside Mrs Roberson's own flat.

'Oh, thank God you're here, Inspector,' said the landlady, her face barely visible by the light of the street lamps. 'The gas has gone off.'

'That's strange,' Maitland remarked. 'The rest of the street still has it. Where's your main gas-tap?'

'Down there to your left,' said Mrs Roberson, above the noise of whimpering behind her. Maitland bent down with a grunt and I heard the squeak of a brass gas-tap being turned.

'Have you turned off all the brackets in your own apartments?' I asked Mrs Roberson.

'Oh yes. But could one of you check upstairs?' The whimpering suddenly stopped.

'Certainly, Mrs Roberson,' my father-in-law said, and proceeded upwards. 'Don't forget Mrs R – no matches, no sparks. And open all your windows down here. You're lucky it's such a warm night.'

'Thank you for your help,' said the landlady. 'You only need to check poor Mr Harrison's flat. There hasn't been anyone in the top apartments for a while. I'll get the key.'

She went into her room and took a key out of some sort of china container, to judge from the sound the key made as it scraped around inside. She handed it to Maitland and returned to her own rooms, while I followed my father-in-law up the stairs. As I caught up with him, he said to me, 'The gas was already off down there. I just moved the valve a bit to make sure. Why would anyone turn it off when there were gaslights blazing away? It's not the sort of thing you could do by accident.'

As we reached the door of what had been Harrison's rooms, I thought I heard a noise inside. I thought it might be a noise from the street, so I didn't mention it to Maitland.

What I saw inside that room would stay in my memory for a very long time. The smell that pervaded the room was equally memorable.

At first I had an absurd impression of snow clinging to various surfaces in the room, such as the angle of the floor beside the unlit fire, and the top of the chair in which Harrison had been found dead. I quickly saw that these drifts of what appeared to be snow were actually the white sheets that Mrs Roberson had used to cover the furniture. These were no longer all on the furniture, but had been taken off and thrown about the room.

Around and on top of these sheets was evidence of a furious and unsystematic ransacking of the flat's contents. The few pieces of furniture had been turned over, the pictures had been thrown on the floor and the shelves of a chest of drawers had been removed and thrown down. I took in all this in a second, before the overpowering presence of coal gas in the room started to make my eyes sting.

I could see every detail in the chaotic room because Isaac Batey was standing with a spirit-lamp at the far end of it. Batey, every inch of whose face was covered with thick dark fur, looked terrifying, lit from below by his own lamp. He looked like some evil creature depicted in a theatre, who creeps downstage to the footlights and chills the blood of the audience.

He was wearing a linen suit, which must at one time have been Harrison's. A heap of prison clothes were lying at his feet. He had a bulging canvas bag on a long strap round his right shoulder.

'Put out that lamp man!' Maitland cried, cowering back behind the door. 'Can't you smell the gas?' I was cowering behind Maitland's considerable bulk, but I was unable to stop myself risking injury by peeping at Batey. Batey gave a chuckle of satisfaction.

'You called me *man*,' he said, exultantly. 'You've finally realised what I am. I'm not some primitive creature. I'm not an animal. I'm just another example of the most terrifying species in creation. All these people swarming over the earth. All these savages and colonisers. Who can tell them apart? But I'm just one of them. I'm a man!'

'Put the lamp out,' Maitland shouted again. The Inspector obviously didn't want to venture too far into the room, for fear of the explosion that he probably guessed was imminent. We both watched round the edge of the door while Batey flung open a window. I wasn't sure if an open window on such a still night would dilute the gas in any way. I suddenly wished I knew more about this invisible substance that is piped into so many houses. I fancied I could hear the gas itself swirling about the room, leaving the grey traces of its residue on every surface.

'Put the lamp out?' Batey said, and, with a slow under-arm swing, he threw the lamp at us.

The lamp, which was a fragile thing of frosted glass blown into modest curves, described a long low arc in that long room, under that high ceiling. It rotated about its centre of gravity, spraying out a thin line of colourless spirit. It seemed to me to hang, stationary, at the top of the arc before it screamed towards the floorboards by the door.

On the floor, it separated itself into discrete components – two colours of glass fragments, a wick, an inner framework of brass, a wave of flailing spirit. A circle of flame spread surprisingly wide over the floorboards before the gas in the air paid it any attention.

The blast slammed the main door of the flat shut. Maitland and myself were thrown backwards by the door, like toy soldiers swept over by a broom. Just before the strong hand of the exploding gas closed the door, I saw Isaac Batey jump head-first out of the window.

Luckily, I landed on Maitland. If his large bulk had landed on me, things might have been very different. I must remark, with admiration, that the detective part of Maitland's brain was still working, even when my elbow was buried deep in the adipose tissue of his abdomen. 'So,' he said, panting with shock, 'there *is* a connection between Batey and this place.'

It seems that the two young uniformed policemen, Robinson and his colleague, were about to re-enter Old Elvet when they heard a terrific bang, followed by the tinkling of glass. They started to run to the corner when Batey ran round it, then ran straight into them. They struggled with him, but he fought, again, with great ferocity. Robinson got a hand on the bag he was carrying, but Batey shrugged the bag off. He ran for Elvet Bridge and threw himself off it and into the river. The policemen started down to the Wear via the alley at the back of the photographer's shop.

Meanwhile, all sorts of people from the neighbouring houses were pouring onto the street. They looked out of place in their evening-round-the-fire clothes: the women in housecoats and the men in smoking-jackets and slippers.

I was curious to know what Maitland would do next. He had seen the two policemen chasing Batey, and there was no point in his joining in: the hunters and their quarry were already out of sight. It was quite possible that Maitland weighed as much as one and a half such fit, young policemen. It was evident to me that he should leave the chasing work to the uniformed officers.

While I wandered about in a daze, wondering stupidly why my ears were ringing, Maitland headed for the gas-taps in Mrs Roberson's hall. He groped about for them and found that the main tap was still turned on. It was somewhat concealed, and in the darkness he had obviously mistaken the tap for the downstairs flat for the tap that could cut off the supply to the whole house. This was easy to do. There was nothing but sixteen inches or so of exposed copper pipe between the two taps, and the taps themselves were identical in everything but their location on the pipe.

Earlier in the evening, someone else had confused the two taps, and with disastrous results. Only an expert with a lantern would have noticed that the pipe conveying gas to the upstairs apartment ran underneath the one which was connected to Mrs Roberson's ground floor rooms. The detective shook his head and smiled the smile of one who suddenly understands everything.

My father-in-law went back out into the street and looked around at the growing crowd of people there. Most were looking up at the windows of Mrs Roberson's first floor, which had been blown out, frames and all. The curtains behind them had been shredded, but I am pleased to say there were no signs of fire. Somebody handed Maitland the bag that had been taken from Batey. He handed it to me.

As I watched, Maitland spotted Adah Harrison and approached her. She was wearing a long burgundy dressing-gown and her hair was loose about her shoulders. She was staring about her, her arms tightly folded. Maitland approached, his large form getting between her and the nearest street-light. The shadow that Maitland cast seemed to consume her or eclipse her. She gazed up at him and drew her arms more tightly about herself. After what looked from a distance like a few serious words, Maitland put his arm round Adah and led her round the corner of Territorial Lane. His arm round her shoulders seemed to express a hot, controlled rage. Where he took her after that, I don't know. I have no idea what he said to her in whatever place they went to, but the events of the next few days gave me some ideas.

I crouched down on my haunches under a street-light and searched through the bag Isaac had been forced to abandon. It contained two shirts, with their collars and cuffs, and shirt-studs in a box.

It also contained the book, the title of which had so puzzled my friend, Basildon Broadlock.

This was the book that I had at first taken to be one of the apocryphal books of Scripture. As it turned out, the Book of Esau, in its original version, was not a printed book at all. It was a book of blank pages, bound in dark blue cloth. Such books can still be purchased at stationers, and are used as diaries, commonplace books, journals, and ledgers or, for the more frivolous owner, for the purpose of writing poetry or novels.

The title appeared on the spine, inscribed in beautiful copperplate handwriting on a square of white paper. This had been glued on. The book was about two-thirds full of the same immaculate handwriting which, in this case, really did look like the lettering used by engravers on copper plates. The writer had left very little space between his lines, or around the edges of the paper, and his writing was very small. Nevertheless it was possible to read the book comfortably, even under a street-light.

The book comprised nothing more nor less than the autobiography of Esau Harrison, written in the form of a series of journal entries over about a decade. While Maitland and Adah were out of sight (I sensed that I should not try to follow them) I stole a first, quick look at The Book of Esau, and began to understand some of its nature and its significance.

When the detective and the widow re-emerged, Adah looked somewhat downcast and frightened. Maitland himself looked as if he had just carried out a very unpleasant duty. He approached a uniformed police sergeant who had run to the scene, having heard the blast. 'I'll be taking Mrs Harrison and Mrs Roberson to my house tonight, Phipps,' he said. 'I want two constables on guard, front and back. Mrs Roberson can stay in the spare bedroom, and Adah can stay in my daughter Hebe's old room. Mrs Harrison is going to appear at Allan Terris's trial tomorrow. She will be a witness for the defence.'

I told Maitland that I thought that the book was important, but he did little more than riffle through the pages. 'This may be useful for the defence as well, young Jacob,' he said. 'You should make a stab at reading through it tonight.'

Chapter XXIII

The next day, I went to Tiger's trial with a much jauntier step, even though I had stayed up all night reading Harrison's book. I could no longer feel the shades of the prison lowering on my mind.

The trial reopened with two surprise witnesses for the defence: Adah Harrison and myself.

I placed The Book of Esau on a corner of the witness stand while I answered Harburton's questions. There were about twenty slips of old newsprint sticking out of it, to mark what I thought would be the parts most relevant to the case.

'Mr Blount,' Harburton began, 'I understand you have been reading a book, hand-written by the supposed murder victim Esau Harrison, which was found near his lodgings last night. Is that correct?'

'It is.'

'How do you know that the book was actually written by Mr Harrison?'

'His name is written on the first page inside. Also, talking to Mrs Harrison just outside, I showed her the book and she confirmed that her husband had written it. She recognised his writing.' Harburton turned to the judge.

'Your honour, Mrs Harrison will confirm that under oath later today.'

'Please proceed,' his honour instructed.

'Mr Blount, what is the nature of this book?' Harburton asked.

'Well, it was originally just a book full of blank pages. I think that Harrison bought it one day with the intention of writing down his life story. He mentions in it that he has published a book before, about all his miracle cures and so forth. Perhaps he thought this one might get into print as well. But I must say, some of it is rather indelicate.' I noticed a sudden stirring of interest among those present in the court.

'Does the book throw any light on Mr Harrison's death?' asked Harburton.

'Well, yes it does. Mostly at the end, I would say.'

'How so?' I hesitated a little.

'As well as living a most interesting life, the late Mr Harrison was also one to entertain some rather unusual notions.'

'Such as?' I scratched my face.

'Unusual notions about the soul, chiefly. I mean, most Christians believe in the soul, but they would probably not grant much credence to Mr Harrison's concept of it. One reads in the Bible of Jesus's casting out of demons. I think that some of those sacred ideas got a little mixed up and embellished in Harrison's mind.'

'In what way?' Harburton asked. 'I don't understand.'

'I suppose the Christian idea is that the soul is joined to the body until death, when it goes to its reward – whatever that reward might be. Now, Harrison seemed to think that *ghosts* exist, and that these are the souls of the departed who are restless in their minds, or have unfinished business.'

'A common enough belief, if one believes in ghosts, surely?'

'Oh yes. But Harrison believed that the soul could also leave the body before death.' There was some muttering about the court. This was indeed an unusual notion. The judge sat up and intervened.

'Is this line of questioning relevant to the actual death of Esau Harrison?'

'I believe so, your honour,' said Harburton. He turned back to me and resumed his questioning

'Mr Harburton,' he began, 'how did Mr Harrison think that the soul could leave the body *before* death?'

'In dreams, for the most part, or even in times of abstraction during the waking hours.

'He also believed that he could communicate directly with the soul of another person, in order to work his miracle cures. He believed that many illnesses considered incurable by conventional medicine could be cured by treating the soul. He also believed that the souls of lovers could mingle. The most relevant thing to this case is that he thought that under certain circumstances the bodies of two people could actually swap souls. I imagine this is something like a man swapping his dwelling, or his clothes, or his occupation, with another man.'

'Extraordinary,' Harburton remarked. 'Did Harrison actually believe that he had ever achieved this 'swap'?' he asked.

'Towards the end of his book, it becomes clear that he believed that it *was* actually happening to him.'

'And who did he think he was swapping souls with?'

'He believed that he was swapping souls with the accused, Allan Terris.' There was an outbreak of concerned muttering about the court, which the judge silenced with a frown.

'Do you think this explains why he was wearing Terris's clothes when he died? And why he shaved off his beard?'

'I do think so. You see, I think *he* thought he was slowly *becoming* Allan Terris.'

'Extraordinary. And by committing suicide, he was effectively murdering Terris, to his own way of thinking?'

'I believe so.'

'Thank you, Mr Blount,' said Harburton. The judge asked counsel for the prosecution if he had any questions.

The prosecution had no questions for me. It had not, after all, had sight of the book.

When Adah Harrison took the witness stand, she gripped the edge of the wooden enclosure as if it was the rail of a ship, and she in a terrible storm. Mr Harburton seemed moved by the tragic beauty of her figure, but swallowed hard and brushed the emotion aside. 'Mrs Harrison,' he said softly.

'Yes?' she said.

'I must commiserate with you for the tragic loss of your husband. My first question to you is, and I must assure you that I ask merely as a matter of form; did you kill your husband?'

'No,' Adah Harrison replied, without seeming to move a muscle of her statuesque form. Harburton waited a moment for the jury to absorb this denial, before continuing.

'Do you think..?

The judge intervened. 'Let us not ask the witness to speculate, Mr Harburton,' he said. 'This case has enough *metaphysical* speculation in it already.'

Harburton apologized, and bit on a joint of his left index finger while he rephrased the question in his head.

'Do you have any reason to believe that Mr Terris, who is on trial here, killed your husband?' Harburton asked.

'Certainly not.'

'Do you think your husband was murdered at all, or by anyone?'

'No. I believe that he committed suicide.' There was a rustle of surprise at the back of the court, and the judge raised an eyebrow at the public gallery.

'I see,' said Harburton. 'Now, I know this must be painful for you, Mrs Harrison, but how did he commit suicide? In your opinion, what was his method?'

'I believe he must have taken an overdose of Laudanum.'

'Laudanum? But there was a bottle of belladonna, that is, deadly nightshade, by him when he died, was there not?'

'Not exactly. It wasn't by his side. The bottle was in the bathroom.'

'Oh yes. But was there not a certain amount of belladonna in the drinking-glass found by his body?'

'He was taking dilute belladonna for his stomach.'

'His stomach?'

'Yes, he had been suffering from colic for several days before he died. He had been in great pain. Belladonna is a good cure for colic. Of course, it has to be taken in great moderation.'

'Yes, but why do you suspect laudanum?'

'Because he had several bottles of laudanum in a box hidden in the fireplace.'

'Now, we know about this supply of laudanum already, don't we? This was the laudanum he was giving to the defendant in smaller and smaller doses?'

'Yes it was.'

'But instead, you say he used it to kill himself.'

'I believe so. Anyway, there was a great deal of laudanum missing when he died'.

'Why would he not just use belladonna?'

'I've thought about this. I'm not a doctor, but

I think laudanum would have been less painful.'

'Yes. We have already heard from Dr Codling in this court about how painful it is to die of belladonna.' Harburton paused as much as he dared. 'Had he seen a physician about his colic?' he asked at last, at the extreme end of his pause.

'No. He never saw doctors.'

'Why not? Couldn't he afford them?'

'No, it wasn't that. He avoided doctors because they always want to examine different parts of one's body, unclothed. Also, they have a natural antagonism toward a man like my husband who cures...I mean cured, people for free, and who used no pills or potions.'

'Except on himself?'

'Yes. He believed some so-called *scientific* medicines had their place. But the illnesses my husband cured with hypnotism were almost always incurable by drugs or operations.'

'You say your husband didn't like to be examined unclothed. It may seem indelicate of me to ask this of a lady like yourself, but surely it is quite normal for a man visiting his doctor to strip to the waist, if asked? I mean, most doctors are men, are they not? And we're all made the same, aren't we?' Adah Harrison flushed red.

'My husband was not,' she said. There was a

sudden silence in the courtroom, followed by an embarrassed laugh, quickly suppressed.

'What do you mean?' asked Harburton, seriously.

'I mean that my husband suffered from hypertrichosis.'

'And what is that?'

'It is also known as hirsutism. It is a condition where the whole body, including the face, is covered with thick fur. Like an ape, or a dog.' At this, the judge stirred irritably and put his own question to Mrs Harrison.

'Don't you think that Dr Codling, who examined the body after death, would have noted this alleged hairiness in his report?'

'My husband shaved his whole body before he killed himself.'

'How do you know that?'

'There was hair all over the bathroom. Much more than usual. Some had gone down the plughole, but there was still quite a lot for me to pick up. This was before my husband died. I thought that this shaving of his whole body was just a caprice of his. I didn't usually do any cleaning around the flat, you understand: Mrs Roberson's daughter Alice did our cleaning, but I didn't want her to see so much hair lying about.' The judge spoke again.

'But I remember seeing your husband in

life,' he said. 'He had a beard, of course. But I don't remember fur *all over* his face!'

'He shaved that. He shaved his forehead, his cheeks and the backs of his hands very carefully three times a day. The hair didn't grow inside the orbits of his eyes or on his ears. Not to an unusual extent, anyway.'

'Please continue,Mr Harburton,' his honour said.

'Thank you, your honour,' said Harburton, bowing slightly. 'Mrs Harrison,' he continued, 'I'm sure you are aware that our fair city of Durham has recently been unwilling host to a man closely resembling your husband. Your husband without the benefit of any shaving, that is.'

'Yes, I was aware of him. I believe he is my husband's son.' This time, there was so much muttering in the court that his honour raised his gavel.

'Really?' Harburton asked.

'His name was given in the papers as IsaacBatey. Batey is I believe the surname of his mother.'

'Then this Isaac Batey is a son of your late husband, by a previous marriage?' Harburton suggested.

'Not a marriage, no.'

'I see. And your husband was aware of the

presence of his son in Durham?'

'Yes. That is what gave him colic. From an excess of anxiety.'

'Why should the presence of his son make your husband anxious?'

'Because he was not a *legitimate* son,' Adah asserted, frankly. 'And because he would neither shave like my husband, nor conceal the circumstances of his birth.'

'So if Batey were to make himself known in Durham, the fact that your husband had had a liaison with this Batey woman, and that he was furry like an animal…'

'These things could have destroyed my husband. Isaac would probably also have revealed the nature of my husband's employment as a young man.'

'What was the nature of that employment, Mrs Harrison?'

'In his youth, my husband had worked as a curiosity, at Melmoth's Circus. Isaac's mother was a fortune-teller in that circus. Of course, such people as fortune tellers have all sorts of traditional tricks that they use to fool the public. In their time together, Miss Batey taught Esau her trade. Later, when he gave up the circus, he decided to used some of the skills Miss Batey had taught him. He began to work as a faith-healer, in America.'

286

'Was Isaac also part of Melmoth's Circus?'

'Yes, but he left the circus when it recently came to Durham, when he heard that his father was living in the city.'

'Ah yes. That was just before our latest flood.'

'Yes.'

'Did you actually meet this Isaac Batey?'

'Yes. Several times. He came to the flat in Old Elvet.'

'And how did Mr Harrison greet his long lost son?'

'He did not greet him at all. He locked himself up in the bedroom and wouldn't come out.'

'Did Batey threaten to expose his father?'

'No. He just wanted to be friends with him. He couldn't remember him at all, from his childhood. I think my husband left Miss Batey as soon as the baby was born. As soon as he saw that the baby was…like him.'

'Did the defendant, Mr Terris, know about the connection between Mr Batey and your husband?'

'No. I'm quite sure he didn't even know what Esau really was, under his clothes.'

Chapter XXIV

Adah's examination by the counsel for the prosecution followed straight after Harburton's very illuminating questioning. The prosecutor tried to make something to his own advantage out of this surprise witness for the defence, but did not get far. He tried to suggest, in his questioning, that Allan and the young Mrs Harrison had fallen in love, and plotted to kill Esau Harrison. In this, the prosecutor seemed to be appealing to that part of the jury who enjoyed saucy plays and ballads about old men with young wives.

Rousing herself from her melancholy trance, Adah answered by upbraiding the distinguished silk in no uncertain terms.

'Do you think I am a loose woman, sir? Do you think I would take up with a drunkard? A laudanum addict? A man who had lived with his father to the age of thirty, and had no prospects, or even a profession any more?' The prosecutor was baffled by this attack, and even stumbled a little behind his desk. 'No further questions, your honour,' he said.

We all waited outside in the air for the verdict. I had been impressed by Adah's testimony, but I was unsure how far the jury would be swayed by it, and in what direction. Much depended on Adah's appearance, it seemed to me, but I wasn't sure how her appearance would affect the men of the jury. If she had had rosy cheeks and blonde ringlets, they would probably have been more deeply moved by what she had said. As it was, her black hair made her look like the wicked woman in some steamy melodrama.

I saw Dr Codling lighting up a cigar and leaning on a pillar in the facade of the courthouse. 'I know what you're thinking,' he said, as I approached him. 'Why didn't that oaf Codling test Esau Harrison for laudanum?'

'I wasn't thinking about that, as it happens. But I suppose it is a reasonable question. Why did you not test for laudanum?'

'I'll tell you why I didn't old chap, and I'll tell you in one word. Pupils.'

'What?'

'The pupils of Esau's eyes. Very large they were, when I examined them. If he'd had laudanum, they should have been tiny, like pinpricks.'

'Is that right?'

'Oh yes. Any kind of opiate will do that, even in a smallish dose.'

'So Harrison cannot have had laudanum?'

'Oh yes he could. But I think he'd also been dosing himself with belladonna. Not just internally, for colic, but externally, from an eyedropper.'

'Really?'

'I think so. Everyone who met him seems to say he had intense, hypnotic eyes. Perhaps he was using deadly nightshade to dilate his pupils and give himself some extra glitter. You know why it's called belladonna, don't you? It means 'beautiful woman'. Women used to drop it in their eyes as a beauty treatment. Some still do. It was the belladonna, on top of the laudanum, that made his pupils so large.

'You know, you can kill a cat with opium and watch its eyes go into pinpricks. If you drop belladonna on its eyes – its dead eyes, mind you – the pupils will dilate.'

'Thank you, doctor,' I said. 'That's one little piece of general knowledge I will not be sharing with my wife.'

Maitland approached us, looking pleased with himself.

'How on earth did you get her to testify?' I asked, though I suspected it was something to do with a certain secret conversation in Territorial Lane.

'She was a good witness, wasn't she?' Maitland said. 'She took no nonsense from that QC.'

'But how did you persuade her?' I asked again.

'She had to testify to keep herself out of prison,' Maitland asserted. 'I know for a certainty that she has helped two men, both believed at some time to be dangerous criminals: Allan Terris and Isaac Batey. She admitted as much to me after the gas explosion. She'd also inadvertently caused that explosion by helping Batey.'

'How do you work that out?' asked Codling, through his cigar smoke.

'She tried to turn the gas off for the whole building so that Batey could sneak in under cover of darkness. But she accidentally turned the gas off for the downstairs flat only. When she did this, the pressure surged in old Harrison's flat upstairs. It was only for a second, but it was more than enough to blow out the gaslights. Batey saw no lights, and he assumed that the gas was switched off in the normal way, so he climbed up into the room from the garden. He managed to light a spirit-lamp up there without any problems because there wasn't much gas in the air. Not yet, anyway. He stole a few mementos of his father and failed to notice the gas smell. That was when we made our timid little entrance, son-in-law.'

Chapter XXV

The Chemical Club of Durham held a party to celebrate the acquittal of Tiger Terris. A large foaming agenda was purchased, and several points of order appeared and were swiftly dealt with. There was much laughter and some comic songs were sung by both Harburton and Terris, that should probably not have been sung so loud. Tiger, and the man who'd worked so hard for his freedom, were now firm friends. They tried to sing a duet, but Harburton's tone-deafness turned the attempt into a disaster. The venue for this celebration was the familiar back room of the Half Moon tavern in New Elvet.

When any other business had been dealt with, I tottered out into the street arm-in-arm with Tiger. Together we slumped over the parapet of Elvet Bridge and watched the water flow under us. I was shocked to notice that Tiger had begun to cry.

'Don' cry. You've bin 'quitted,' I reminded him.

'I know, Jacob,' he said mournfully.

'Then why you cryin'?'

'Have you heard about Adah?' he asked, gazing down into the black river.

'Of course.'

'Gone to live with that Batey fellow. In old Mochnacki's house. Going to marry Batey, apparently.'

'So I've heard.'

'By why would that old Polish chap give them a place to live?'

'Without knowing it,' I said, 'the Pole and Adah had something in common before they even met.'

'What was that?'

'Mochnacki was leaving a tray out for Batey. And Adah was buying meat pies for him, and taking them to him down by the river.'

'So they say,' said Terris, in a very melancholy voice. 'But what has Mochnacki got in common with *him*, with the hairy chap?'

'I think I know the answer to that,' I said. 'Mochnacki came here to England to escape the hard times his people were having over in Poland. He is Jewish, you know, from his father's side.'

'Oh yes,' Terris agreed.

'Well, some places treat Jews like monsters,

like chimeras...'

'I see. Mochnacki is sheltering someone who is a bit out of the ordinary, because he is a bit out of the ordinary himself.'

'That's what I think,' I said. 'And Adah's done wonders with the house apparently.' There was a pause while we watched the river below us.

'She offered herself to me,' Terris said then, his mouth close to my ear, 'she offered herself to me. But she didn't really want me. That's why I didn't take her. I'd had enough of that sort of thing in the army'

'You pushed her away?'

'That's right. She didn't want me. You know what she wanted?'

'No.'

'David and Bathsheba,' he said, and turned to go.

I watched Tiger for a few minutes, tottering along the street, back to his father's house, his back very straight.

We kept our Bible next to our volumes of Shakespeare and Tennyson, in the bedroom. I undressed and lay down beside Hebe's sleeping form, using the italic page headings to find my way through the King James Version to David and Bathsheba.

Bathsheba it was who caught the eye of King David when he saw her bathing one night from the battlements of his palace. She was a childless married woman: childless because of the indifference of her husband Uriah. I could see the application to Adah Harrison's case. Desperate for a child, she found that her husband would not give her one. Why? Because his first, illegitimate, child had been unnaturally hirsute like himself. He didn't want another like that. Their marriage remained unconsummated. But she turned to Tiger, because she wanted to give Esau a normal child.

That's what she wanted with him. Esau Harrison probably knew what was happening under his own roof. Ashamed, angry, sympathetic, isolated, he became confused. If only I could be Allan Terris, he thought. *If only my soul could change bodies with his.*

In his very modern bathroom, he set about shaving off all the hair on his body that he could reach. He stood in the bath to do this, and washed the loose hairs off with the shower. The only place he could not reach was that place where the hair of someone with hypertrichosis grows thickest – on the top half of the back.

Having even shaved off his beard, he dressed in Tiger's clothes, stolen from Tiger's room. He now believed that he *was* Tiger, having quite transformed himself. Tiger's soul inhabited his form, and Harrison's translated body started to feel Tiger's lust for laudanum. He took a mighty swig from one of the bottles hidden in the fireplace, then staggered to the chair in which he would soon die.

Unused to the drug, Harrison was quickly overcome. No doubt his heart gave out, as his mind plunged into dark, terminal laudanum dreams. Tiger found him dead, and fled in panic, believing that he would be blamed. Longing for the opiate, he could not resist taking one of the metal boxes at Harrison's feet. It was probably open, and it contained some laudanum at least. This was the metal box I had seen in Tiger's 'nest' at Old Canch.

I never asked Tiger what that box contained, or what he did with the contents. I would like to think that he poured what was undoubtedly laudanum into one of the drains at Old Canch. The other boxes that had lain at the feet of Harrison contained a great deal of money, in Stirling and in American dollars. This money was impounded by the police as evidence in the Terris murder trial. I understand that Adah Harrison claimed it from the police before she went to live with Mochnacki and Isaac Batey. Mrs Roberson did not press charges against Batey for having entered her flat, and the other charges against him were dropped, once his story was known.

The morning after our celebration at the Half Moon, having soothed my head with a strong cup of coffee laced with brandy, I took a stroll along Old Elvet. In the hardening light, I saw the workmen taking out what they could from the damaged parts of Mrs Roberson's house.

There were piles of curtains cut to ribbons, a tea-chest of brass fittings and the pieces of a smashed wardrobe. In the midst of this stuff, sitting on the kerb, was a boy forcing a pipe cleaner down a copper pipe. From the other end came a tube of damp, compacted hair.

Harburton consulted his law-books, and found that Adah could legally marry her step-son, since her relations with Esau Harrison had never amounted to a marriage in the fullest legal sense. After a quiet wedding at which Tiger Terris and myself were proud to be witnesses, this strange couple continued to live with Mochnacki.

Historical note

Joseph Boruwlaski, the 'Little Count', was a real resident of Durham: some of his personal effects can still be seen in a display case in the old County Hall. His supposed 'house' remains as a picturesque folly down by the Wear. His Jewish nephew, Mochnacki, is an invention of mine.

Old Elvet and New Elvet are real streets in the city. Old Elvet leads straight up to the city's law courts and the prison. The medieval building on Elvet Bridge where the fictional Blounts had their photographic business is now part of a restaurant.

For free downloads and more from the Langley Press, please visit our website at http://tinyurl.com/lpdirect.

www.ingramcontent.com/pod-product-compliance
Lightning Source LLC
Chambersburg PA
CBHW020915200626
46814CB00001BA/355